Other Novels by Heather Neff

Blackgammon

Wisdom

Accident of Birth

This one's for you, Michael

. . . like the very cup of trembling

Acknowledgments

Many years ago I purchased a tattered copy of James Baldwin's *The Fire Next Time* in a used bookstore on the Rue La Fayette in Paris. I had never read any Baldwin, and I remember the sense of excitement I felt when I curled up with the book in my room on the Avenue Jean Jaurès that gray winter day.

I had grown up in the midst of the civil rights movement and had often heard Baldwin's name mentioned in tandem with Black leaders such as Julian Bond, Andrew Young, Ralph Abernathy, and the great Dr. King. In my mind, James Baldwin was inextricably tied to historic events such as the March on Washington. He was, in a sense, one of the Founding Fathers of modern Black America.

At twenty-two years old I had left the United States, filled with a deep and inarticulate sadness about our nation's continuing racial strife. I had come to France in the hope of finding spiritual solace, but I soon felt a great longing for the African-American culture of my homeland. This desire led me to Baldwin's writing.

It would be difficult for me to describe just how deeply I was moved by *The Fire Next Time*. Perhaps it is sufficient to say that in the ensuing weeks I purchased and read every book by Baldwin that I could find. A few years later I wrote a graduate thesis on James Baldwin's novels and essays; I eventually became a professor and found myself in the fortunate position of being able to share his work with the next generation of readers.

I cannot fully describe the debt that my novel *Haarlem* owes to James Baldwin's extraordinary short story "Sonny's Blues." I have never read another author who captures the urgent mixture of love and despair that is characterized by the brothers in Baldwin's masterpiece. Like Baldwin, I, too, have turned to the Bible for the archetypical stories that mirror so many of our present-day human dilemmas. And like Baldwin, I find myself moved to examine the terrible forms of self-destruction that haunt our communities—perhaps in response to our continuing rage at being, as Baldwin put it, "the disesteemed."

I would like to dedicate this book to my brother, Michael Gregory Mayson, whose courage as a writer continues to inspire me, and whose search for his own truth never falters.

My thanks in the preparation of this manuscript go to my ever-patient and supportive husband, Marcel Neff, our deeply loved daughter, Aviva, and my perceptive and encouraging friend, Tanisha Bailey.

I also wish to extend my thanks to my editor at Broadway Books, Clarence Haynes, and to both Tracy Jacobs and Janet Hill, executive editor of Harlem Moon, for supporting this project to completion.

haarlem

I f she'd loved me, she wouldn't have named me Abel."

"What do you mean?"

"I mean that nobody in their right mind needs to be named after a sheep boy."

"I kinda like it. Reminds me of Honest Abe."

"Naw, man. That comes from Abraham. Abel is that nobody with nothing to think about except cutting up dumb animals to please that invisible white man in the sky. 'Please, Mister Lord—please accept my humble offering.' Then crack! He gets beat down by his own brother. Jeesus. I might as well be named Clark Kent. Or Moby-Dick. Or Pinocchio."

"No way, buddy. Abel is a guy who gets things done. Like, he's capable. He's got abil-ity. He's able-minded."

"Or maybe he's just disabled!"

"Look, man, you need to cut yourself a little slack."

"Why is that, Serge? Nobody else ever did—"

Sweet Jesus! I hate planes. Can't smoke. Can't stand the food. Can't sleep. So there's nothing to do but think. Think about conversations that lead to nothing, to questions that'll never be answered. Or about things that need to be buried deep down beneath the earth.

Buried with my not-soon-enough forgotten past.

Buried with my loving father.

And with my Thirst.

My seat above the wing was too damn noisy to let me get any shut-eye. Every time I tried to let myself go, a crash from the galley or a lurch of turbulence would slap me back to reality. Who knew what was going on back there? Could be some asshole with a box cutter or a bomb in his shoe.

Stomach turning over, I stared up the aisle at the passengers' drooping heads until my eyes fastened on the flight attendant's ass, appearing and disappearing behind the first-class curtain. Well, at least *that* was a nice little show.

I was aching for one of those palm-sized gin bottles and a Newport.

"*No shit,*" I thought, continuing my imaginary conversation with Serge. "*If she hadn't given me this stupid name I wouldn't even be on this goddamn plane. Wouldn't have spent that couple of bricks left over from the funeral to buy a ticket to a place where I know I don't need to go. Wouldn't be using up my hard-earned vacation looking for a woman who doesn't even care if I'm alive.*"

"*You got something better to do?*"

"*You damn straight! I should be in Vegas this very minute sitting by a roulette wheel.*"

"*Come on, Abe. You don't know a goddamn thing about gambling!*"

"*I might have a hidden talent. Might turn out to be a crack at the tables.*"

"*A crackhead, more likely.*"

"*Might even strike it rich!*"

"*And then what?*"

"*No more stinking tunnels, man. No more busted cables at four a.m. No—I'd just take my ass to a bamboo hut in the Bahamas and never be seen again.*"

"*The Bahamas? Oh, please! You hate fishing, you can't swim and you sure as hell don't need a tan.*"

"*So I'd write my book, Serge. Write from sunrise to sunset, live off mangoes and papayas and let the paper make some sense out of my goddamn life.*"

"*That's crazy, Abe. How're you gonna live without your daily dose of Miles?*"

"*I'd just get me some steel drums and teach the natives how to play them Harlem-style.*"

I tried to imagine myself, naked and dreadlocked, surrounded by West Indian beauties in my thatched hut by the sea, but the plane's engines forced me back to my New York reality: night after night of dragging cables through the tunnels beneath the city, my bones aching from the constant grind of the generators. The only difference between my shifts in the tunnels and this long damn flight was that now I was strapped into a plane seat, so I couldn't get up and piss a hot stream into a dark alley. No, on a plane you were trapped in a space even smaller than a coffin.

Smaller than my own father's coffin.

"Planes is cool, boy," he used to say every time he spotted a silver bird rising into the sky from La Guardia. "Planes take you away to some other life. Get you out of the ghetto. Take you somewhere where it don't matter if you Black. Ain't no Jim Crow on a plane. Seats all the same size. Tinfoil food same for every damn body. Liquor, too."

Liquor. My hands began to tremble at the thought of a whisky sour at thirty-three thousand feet. *Lick. Er.* Sweat slicked my forehead and my finger inched toward the little orange silhouette of a woman on the armrest. All I'd have to do was press the button. Press the button. A lovely, melodic *blink* would sound and that blonde with the nice ass would pad over to my seat. She'd bend over, her breasts near my cheek, and smile.

"Can I get you something, sir?"

I would look up into her eyes and ask for just one teeny-tiny little something to hold me over the Atlantic.

"Chivas? Tanqueray? Or Beefeater, sir?"

"Make it a Chivas."

Yessir. She'd nod and vanish up the aisle, then reappear with a small white tray and a plastic tumbler filled with rock-hard ice and a blue cocktail napkin. I'd thank her and lean back, gently twisting the cap off the little palm-size bottle. Smiling secretly, I'd play a little roulette with my choice of poison, pouring a perfect arc of golden liquid into that plastic glass. Then I'd take a sip, feeling my tongue go numb under the smooth assault of the scotch. With stunning slowness I would drink my medicine, letting the icy lava roll down like a slow-motion orgasm from my scalp to my toes. Might even put me to sleep like the businessman on my left, who began to snore, his breath smelling like booze, even before the vulture took off.

"Easy does it, man," I heard Serge's warning voice: "You got to fight to control it. When it tickles your balls, ignore it. When it aches in your heart, speak to it. But when it starts screaming in your brain, that's when you got to call on your Higher Power—"

"I don't need a Higher Power!"

"Come on, Abe. You been dealing with this long enough to know you can't do it alone."

"But I am alone. And I got to deal with it alone."

"Look: Your sobriety is too damned important to get fucked up by your pride."

"What the fuck is that supposed to mean?"

"Just because you hate your father doesn't mean you have to hate God. . . ."

"Sheeit," I muttered, stroking the tiny orange button, but not hard enough to illuminate it. Once again I caught a glimpse of the flight attendant's blue uniform, and my thoughts leapt to another uniformed woman—the nurse in the intensive care unit, called by the blinking buttons on my father's life-support system.

Green, blue, yellow flashing buttons. How could anyone stand the thought that one touch on the wrong button might literally end somebody's life? I thought about that Black woman's vibe. She looked mighty comfortable as she checked monitors and adjusted gauges.

"Does he feel anything?" I asked her, trying to replace the low moan of those machines with a human voice. The nurse glanced over at me, shook her head without speaking, and left the room.

I only realized when the door swished shut behind her that my father, Louis Franklin Crofton—one of the biggest mother-fuckers of all time—was finally going to die.

They'd wanted to put him into hospice, but his condition went down so fast that they'd ended up just letting him fade out in the same three-by-six space where the ambulance spat him out two days earlier. An emergency call had found its way through the network of public service offices and switchboards of assistants and managers until my shift captain heard a crack-ling voice on the radio. The cap walked through the November night and climbed down the steel ladder to the tunnel below Seventh Avenue.

"Crofton!" His voice echoed down to where we were rewiring the city's electric grid in a floodlit manhole. Thinking that Nee Cee had found some new way to drive me crazy, I climbed up, cursing under my breath while the other guys muttered, "Shit, she's at it again!" and "Can't Abe muzzle that bitch?"

But instead of the hysterical ranting of my once-upon-a-sometime woman, I heard a cold voice on the line, telling me about Louis Crofton's collapse at some run-down nightclub. He needed surgery immediately.

I traveled to the hospital by subway, still wearing my work clothes, my boots crusty with mud. I hardened my heart against the painful memories as the train rocketed up to Harlem. And finally I stood in the center of a ring of doctors who told me that my father's liver was shot and he had nothing left to do but die.

Reluctantly I called Nee Cee and asked her to go to my place and bring me some fresh clothes. I tried not to think about the fact that she would ransack every inch of my apartment for any sign of a female presence. I knew she'd find the condoms and the number of the girl from the building next door who came up for a recreational fuck every once in a while. Nee Cee would also discover that stash of videocassettes and the couple of worn-out magazines I couldn't bring myself to throw out.

But Nee Cee's jealousy was the price I'd have to pay. I wanted to stay by Louis's side in case he said something. Standing in the antiseptic hall while nurses walked by, I figured that this was my last chance to know.

And my wish was granted—at least in part. Sometime in the middle of the second day my father asked for water. I scrambled across the room from the window where I'd been watching the gray buildings and the gray sky and the gray traffic below. I crouched beside him, taking what I could of his swollen fingers into my hand and leaning in close.

"This is some shit," Louis declared through all the medications.

"You're doing good, Dad," I muttered, almost ashamed of myself for such an outright lie.

"Don't waste your breath," he hissed. He tried to shift, but the straps and tubes held him tight. "Listen, boy, I want you to give Vanelle my mama's Bible," he said clearly. I felt his thick flesh shake in my hand. "Go and get my horn from the club. That's for your Uncle Buddy." There was a long pause. "Everything else is for you."

Silence followed. I didn't know what to say because I knew damn well there wasn't much else. I had never in my life gotten a goddamn thing from my father—except maybe my addiction to alcohol and my love of jazz.

Now he grunted heavily and closed his eyes. I brought my face down to his lips.

"Pop?" I whispered, daring myself to do what forty-five years on earth hadn't given me the guts to do. "Pop—do you know where she is?"

For a minute I thought he hadn't heard me. Or that he just wasn't going to answer. Then his eyes opened to slits and I caught a glimpse of the sly man I'd known for all of my life.

"I don't give a shit where she's at."

"I—I need to find her."

"She don't want you."

"Pop, if you know, please tell me," I said, strangling on the respect I was giving him.

"Far as I know—" Louis managed to turn his head—"she long since gone."

"At least—at least tell me her name."

The yellow eyes fixed on my face. "She don't have no name."

Those words hit me like a slap in the face. I dropped his hand and sat back on the chair beside the bed. I knew I should say something more to him. Something about God. But I couldn't.

Finally I stood up. My anger felt like lead in the soles of my shoes. I stood looking down on the mummified figure until I realized he was no longer breathing.

Suddenly I was jolted awake by the voice of the captain notifying the passengers that we were beginning our descent into Amsterdam's Schiphol International Airport. I glanced around, realizing that I had managed to fall asleep—in fact, I'd slept right through my breakfast. The flight attendants were coming up the aisles, throwing the plastic trays into dark garbage bags. I felt like spitting to clear the airplane taste from my mouth. I felt like pissing, but the line to the bathrooms stretched nearly to the front of the plane.

Well, I made it. All the way to the Netherlands. And I managed to do it without pushing that orange button.

You're right, Serge, I thought as the seat-belt light flashed on. Easy does it.

I followed the groggy line of passengers down a corridor toward Passport Control.

"What is the purpose of your trip?" The immigration officer looked at my passport.

I'm looking for a woman without a name, I thought. "Vacation," I said.

The man looked up. "How long do you plan to be here, Mr. Crofton?"

Not a moment longer than necessary. "Ten days."

For a long, cool moment he looked into my eyes and I wondered what this white man saw: A drunk? A tunnel worker? A Black man who had no right to be here?

"Enjoy your stay," he said, snapping my passport shut and nodding me through the gate.

Shouldering my bag, I crossed the glass-and-steel terminal. This was it: my first view in memory of the world outside the United States. Hell—this was my first view of life beyond New York.

Soon the taxi was winding through Amsterdam's needle-thin streets, which were crowded with bicycles and parked cars. Every street seemed to border a canal, and the canals were full of houseboats and barges.

"The Netherlands was once only marshland," the taxi driver explained. I was surprised by how good his English was. "That is, of course, the reason our nation is called the 'Netherlands'— or 'low countries.' Our forefathers created our nation by building these waterways and constructing dikes against the sea."

Dikes? An image of the little blond boy in wooden shoes with his finger stuck in the wall flashed through my mind, but it was instantly replaced by the sight of a series of bridges rising in parallel arches over yet another canal. I'd secretly collected pictures of Amsterdam when I was a kid, tearing them out of magazines in the school library and hiding them under my mattress at home. But now I was surprised at how much more beautiful Amsterdam was than the photos—even in December. The taxi turned onto a narrow waterfront street.

"We are now entering the oldest part of the city," the driver continued. "Many of these buildings date back to the sixteenth century. They were constructed by wealthy merchants. You can see the—how do you say it?—the pulleys on the top floor of the buildings. They were once used to unload goods from boats docked below."

Damn smart. Build your city so you can move the goods by boat directly to the merchant's door. Have fresh water flowing right in front of the houses. Connect everything up with bridges.

Tall brick houses with rows of windows looked out over the

water. Christmas lights were strung along the window frames and doorways. I noted that there were no security bars on any of the windows or doors—not even at ground level.

"And that is the Rijksmuseum," the driver said as we passed a big stone building. "Many artistic treasures of the Dutch people are on display there. And the Van Gogh Museum is just a few doors away, behind that park. I hope you will have the opportunity to visit them."

I prefer a different kind of art, I thought as I caught sight of a chick in some tights jogging over a bridge. The taxi stopped at a red light just beside the Amstel brewery. Its giant Heineken sign, decorated with a glowing neon wreath, winked at me.

"Of course, one can also take a tour of the beer factory."

The driver was observing me in the rearview mirror.

"That's cool," I said. That's fucked up, I thought, forcing myself to look away.

The morning light filtered through the trees, still clinging to the last of their leaves. There was a low-level city-roar, but it was just a hum in comparison to New York.

"So you are spending the holidays with us?"

"Excuse me?"

"Well, as it is only one week until Christmas, I thought that perhaps you came to Amsterdam for the holiday."

Hell, no. "Yes. Absolutely."

"Our city is very festive during this season," he went on. "We serve many traditional foods and pastries and enjoy visiting Christmas markets."

"Christmas markets?"

"Yes. They are open-air markets where women sell crafts they have made throughout the year."

"How nice."

The light changed and the taxi moved forward. In the distance I could see a large harbor with ships bearing the logo of Royal Dutch Shell. A few minutes later we rolled to a stop.

"We're here, sir."

"What, already?" I glanced out the window at a brown brick building with dark windows, facing—yeah, another canal.

"Yes, sir. This is your hotel."

"Looks like a factory to me."

"It's one of the oldest buildings in Amsterdam," the driver explained as he turned off the engine. "It was a guild house built by textile merchants in the sixteenth century. I believe it was renovated only a few years ago."

I fumbled with the brightly colored euros, slightly pissed that I didn't know how much to tip.

"I hope you enjoy your stay," the driver murmured as he set my small bag on the curb. He handed me a business card. "Feel free to call me if you need a ride back to the airport."

The taxi drove off and I took a look around. More of those tall houses with pulleys on the roof stretched off in both directions. A footbridge led to a modern building on the opposite bank. Even though it was late December, the air was mild. As the sun rose, I could see the sky was going to be mostly gray.

So this was Amsterdam.

A young cat in a uniform turned up, hoisting my single bag onto a luggage cart and leading me into the lobby. The place had a low, beamed ceiling and was filled with flowers. As I waited for my key I noticed that a Christmas scene with small porcelain figurines was set up on a table beside the front desk. The angels, animals, and holy family were white, but one of the Three Kings was Black. Now, why was that?

"This is your first trip to our city?" the porter asked as we rose to the hotel's fifth floor in the smallest damn elevator I'd ever seen.

"Actually, I was born here."

"Then welcome home, sir."

Leading me into my room, he pulled back the curtains and turned on the lights. I had never seen anything like it: porcelain vases of purple tulips were placed on the table and dresser. A king-size bed covered with a gold-threaded spread that matched the curtains. And the bathroom was tiled in white marble.

It made the motels where I used to take my women look like Attica.

"The television is here, sir." He opened a cabinet in the corner. "The minibar is below." He pointed to soft drinks, bottled water, and airline-sized shots of gin, scotch, and bourbon. "A complimentary breakfast is served between six and ten-thirty every morning, and the hotel restaurant is open from eleven a.m. until ten o'clock at night. Will you be needing anything else at this time?"

I need you to take everything in that goddamn minibar with you.
"No thanks."

"Then everything is to your satisfaction?"

"Sure," I mumbled, realizing that he was fishing for his tip. I handed him a bill peeled from my roll of strange-looking money. He asked me to enjoy my stay and I was finally alone.

I walked slowly to the window, pushed open the double panes, and leaned out into the December morning, taking in the rooftops and the canal below. I stood there for a while, hoping to get some sense of Amsterdam's secret music. Would it be Mingus, like Harlem after midnight? Or maybe Dizzy, the way midtown Manhattan moved in the afternoon? I searched for a rhythm—some kind of a melody on the breeze.

All I saw was wet tiles and dark water.

There I stood, my New Yorker's eyes struggling to look at a skyline with no skyscrapers, my soul terrorized by a city with no sound. Wheeling around, I snatched up the remote and stabbed at the buttons until I was saved by Bugs Bunny speaking Dutch. For a few moments I stared gratefully at the screen. At least *something* seemed a little bit like home.

Finally, not knowing what to do, I sat down on the bed and dropped my head into my hands. I had come so far that I couldn't admit, even to myself, that this was probably nothing but another crash landing.

"What'll it be?"

The waitress appeared from a back room, a wire rack of glasses in her arms. She set the rack in the sink, wiped her hands, and gave me a chance to enjoy the view.

And the view was nice, too: ginger skin, black eyes and a curly-nappy deep brown 'fro. Reminded me of Flora, a Brazilian chick I dated back home—her face a jigsaw of Black and Spanish and even some Mayan. Long-waisted. High, ripe breasts. Like those girls on the beaches in Rio. This one even moved like a samba.

"Coffee. As black as you got."

She jerked a handle with a slender arm and filled a tiny cup with espresso. She was wearing a black sweater and a short black leather skirt. Her hair corkscrewed over dark, street-smart eyes.

She was perfect for the place where she worked—Café Vetiver—a kind of bar-cum-coffeehouse just around the corner from my hotel. Located on the ground floor of an old row house, the inside was brightened by wide windows that faced—that's right, another canal. Black leather sofas and armchairs lined the rear wall, but I was seated solo at a glass-brick counter facing a smoked mirror. The woman placed the cup on a saucer and slid the java toward me.

I lit a Newport and studied myself in the mirror, somewhat surprised at the face that stared back. My cheeks appeared to be cut at sharp angles, and my eyes, usually cautious, seemed strangely peaceful. Especially considering the fact that everything around me was the unknown.

My hair was growing back from the buzz cut I'd worn to Louis's funeral a month earlier. The black curls rose away from my forehead and nearly reached my collar. I'd shaved carefully, leaving a light beard to shade in my chin and jaw.

"First time in Amsterdam?" The waitress was rinsing ashtrays as she spoke.

"In a way."

"Like it?"

I shrugged, letting a curl of smoke pour out of my mouth. "What I've seen."

Pushing that thick mane away from her eyes, she looked me over quickly. "Business?"

"Tourist."

"You're out of season."

"Cheaper fares."

"Lousy weather."

"Doesn't matter."

She turned the water off with a flick of her elbow. "Sight-seeing?"

"A little bit."

"Looking for something?"

"Not really."

"Someone?"

I paused. "What makes you ask that?"

She dried her hands on a towel and leaned back against the sink, crossing those nice breasts with her long arms. "Well, let's see: No briefcase. No camera. No tourist books. No maps and no business suit. You don't even have a shopping bag. So what's left?"

"Maybe—" I drew on my cigarette—"I'm a spy."

"No dark glasses."

"Plenty of bases in Germany. I could be AWOL."

"No. You look like you're hunting. Not being hunted."

I laughed and the sound surprised me. It had been a while since anything seemed truly funny. I looked her over again. And then I saw it: beneath that sexy-cool was a black crystal polished to a rocklike hardness.

"That was quite an observation."

"I see a lot from back here."

"Then tell me where I'm from."

"New York. Maybe Chicago."

"Why not L.A.?"

"You're dressed just right for this weather. And you don't look like you surf."

"So what do you think I do?"

"Well"—the tip of her tongue traveled to the swell of her lips—"teachers don't travel just before Christmas. Rich guys don't come into little places like this. And poor guys are always looking for—how do you say it? A hustle."

"So what does that make me?"

Her eyes went to my hands, which were chapped and scarred from years of labor beneath concrete. "A workingman, I think. And I think a man who works at night."

"Because?"

"Because you look like you'd rather be asleep right now."

"Maybe it's just jet lag. Or maybe"—I teased her with my eyes—"I'm part vampire."

"Impossible," she replied, glancing toward the canal outside. "I know a monster when I see one."

Shaking my head, I took a sip of the strong black coffee. "Where'd you learn such good English?"

"Men. Music. Life."

"In that order?"

She took in a deep breath. "That depended on the day of the week."

"Sounds depressing," I said, drawing hard on my cigarette.

She shrugged. "Sounds like life to me." She looked out the window again.

Several people rode by on bicycles. The café was almost empty and I wanted to keep her talking.

"So what's life like in this place?"

"Like everywhere else, I guess."

"You been here long?"

"Seventeen years, more or less."

"Then you must like Amsterdam."

"I'm used to it."

I tried to guess her age, but her face and body put her any-where between eighteen and thirty-five.

"What if," I said casually, "I *was* looking for someone?"

"What do you mean?"

"Where would I start?"

"The phone book."

"No luck. Already tried in the hotel."

She looked calmly into my eyes. "The police."

I shifted uncomfortably. The cops were never a Black man's friend, whether he was in Amsterdam, Harlem or the reaches of Outer Mongolia. When I didn't respond she spoke again. "Maybe for you it's better to go to the Bevolkings Register."

"The what?"

"The Family Registry. You're searching for a relative, aren't you?"

"Why would you say that?"

The woman slowly unhooked her arms, reaching out to brace herself against the counter. "You know, Amsterdam has always been a city of escape. Many people arrive here from all over the world. So many other people come here to find them."

The bar door opened and several customers entered, greeting the waitress in Dutch. She returned to her work, filling glasses of beer and sliding clean ashtrays over the counter. I didn't want to look at those foaming glasses of beer, so instead I watched her ass as she moved back and forth in that leather skirt. The other men in the café were getting an eyeful, too.

When she finished I asked her for directions to the Registry. She took out a napkin and a pen and drew a map, pointing out the main train station, my hotel and our present location.

"They're probably open until six," she said. "Do you speak any Dutch?"

I shook my head.

"Well, someone there should speak English."

"Why did you ask me if I speak Dutch?"

"You're Dutch, aren't you?"

"I'm Black."

"So what?"

"I'm from America."

"But you have Dutch blood."

"How do you know?"

She smiled ironically. "What's your name?"

"Abel."

"Full name?"

"Abel Paulus Crofton."

"Crofton?" She lifted her head so that her hair fell away from her eyes. "Your father was the American. So you, Abel Paulus, are looking for your mother."

———

Abel Paulus Crofton really *is* a stupid name. And it sounds even stupider on a Black man. One day, in a rare moment of bourbon-induced civility, Louis explained to me that it was the custom in the Netherlands to name boys after saints.

"There ain't no saint named Abel," I grumbled.

"Naw," my father laughed. "But she liked that name."

"Why?"

"Because of that story in the Bible."

"The story about them two brothers?"

"How the fuck you know that?"

"Grandma told me. She said God liked one of them but he was mad at the other one. Then the bad one killed his brother and lied about it. But why my mama give me a name like that?"

His face closed, as it always did when I got too close to some kind of truth. "She stupid."

"That why she spelled my other name wrong?"

"It ain't spelled wrong. That's the way they spell it in their language."

"Paul-us?" I asked sullenly. "Why you let her name me that?"

" 'Cause you stupid, too."

It seemed that everybody at P.S. 182 agreed with him. I got my butt kicked regularly for being the Black boy whose hair wound up in thick Puerto Rican curls, along with my milk-coffee skin. And my light brown eyes labeled me for a fag long before I even knew what a fag was. Tall and skinny, I tried to avoid the stares of cops who mistook me for a man when I was still a boy. I couldn't shake my runner's build or hide the long fingers that ignited the pilot lights in store clerks' eyes.

And if my face wasn't strange enough, I still had to live down my stupid, stupid name.

Louis Crofton shared my classmates' distaste, snarling whenever I entered the room. To get away, I often escaped to the edges of Harlem, where I wondered at the elegant brownstones lining the East River. Sometimes I sat on the curb for hours, staring into the dark waters. I ignored the men in shining cars that pulled up beside me and blew the horn. And I flinched when the women in thigh-high boots appeared, running their plastic nails through my hair.

The only real love I ever knew came from my grandmother, who kept our two-room tenement spotless, filling it with a southern perfume of collard greens and ham hocks and the thrilling voice of Mahalia from her crackling old radio. I still remember the dizzying smoke of burning candles as she prayed that her sax-playing son Louis wouldn't be knifed in some drunken barroom dispute. And that her grandson Abel would grow up to be a better man than his father.

"You got to stay in school, baby," she'd say as she tucked me into my cot in the hall. "Read every book you can find and learn everything the white man know."

"Why do I have to do that?"

"Because Black men need to know everything about being Black and being white, too."

"But I'm not white, Grandma."

"I know, sugar. But I want something better for you when you grow up."

"Ain't I good enough?" I asked and she looked down at me with sadness in her eyes.

"Sweet Jesus," she said in her gentlest voice, "I been cleaning white people's houses for forty years in the hope that my children wouldn't have to live like this. I don't know what went wrong with your daddy. But I go to sleep every night praying you won't end up slaving in New York 'til the end of your days."

"If you been praying so long, why don't God do something?"

"Maybe God want us to try to do it for ourself."

"Then why do we need God?"

"Because sometime we just can't make it on our own."

"What do it mean to 'make it,' Grandma?"

"It don't necessarily mean that you rich, baby. It just mean that you don't owe nothin' to nobody. It mean that you stay away from the bottle and the needle. It mean that you can look in the mirror and feel respect for the person you see."

"But I don't look like nobody."

"Of course you do, baby. You look like yourself."

"But that's not enough, Grandma. I want to look like you or Daddy."

"You will when you grow up, sugar. Just give it time."

It got dark early. I wasn't too cool with standing in the shadows just down the block from Café Vetiver. But there I was, waiting for the waitress to end her shift. She had told me that her name was Sophie, and I felt slightly ashamed that less than twelve hours after arriving in Amsterdam I was already trying to hit on a chick.

She showed up just after five, her stuff in a leather backpack and a rust-colored shawl wrapped around her shoulders. As she approached, weaving her way through cyclists in business suits, I noted that her eyes were now rimmed with black eyeliner. She'd also ripened those lips with a nice shade of copper.

"Hey," I said as she passed me.

She glanced up and her face tightened. "Yes?"

"Could you give me directions again to that office? I think I lost the map you made for me this morning."

You're full of shit, she said with her eyes. "I'm going in that direction," she said with her mouth. "You can come with me."

She took off at a jackhammer pace, leading me through the rush-hour crowds without looking back. I settled in just behind her, glad for a little bit of company—even if I knew I was on borrowed time.

Amsterdam was turning out to be nothing like Manhattan. The streets were so orderly and the people so polite that it seemed like a small town in comparison. And though I'd spent the better part of that afternoon trying to get some sense of who these folks were, I had to admit to myself that I was still lost. Nothing in Amsterdam was really jiving with me.

We stopped on a corner to let a streetcar pass and I took a good look at Sophie. Though she was a small woman—I guessed about five foot three—her legs were shapely beneath that melon-shaped behind. With those full breasts and her tiny waist, she was the finest thing in sight.

"You waitress full-time?"

She barely turned her head. "Yes."

"You work out?"

"Work out?"

"Exercise. Sport. Like going to the gym or something."

"No."

"You look like maybe you're a dancer."

"I'm not a dancer."

And Black guys don't turn you on, I thought as she set off again. You've probably never even been with a Black man before.

I caught our reflection in a window and made myself a bet on how long it would take me to change that. At six foot four, with shoulders stacked from years of lugging cable through the depths of the city, I was used to getting pretty much any woman I wanted. Or didn't want. Nee Cee was, in fact, just the latest in a long line of sisters who stayed around even though I made it clear it wasn't going anywhere.

Sophie and I crossed a courtyard lined with restaurants and cafés and I heard a saxophone wail from the open door of a building. CLUB COLTRANE was written in neon letters above the entrance.

"It's kind of early for a nightclub, isn't it?"

"They're probably rehearsing."

"Are they any good?"

"Some people think so."

"Where are we right now?"

"This is the Rembrandtsplein."

Sanctuary, I thought, glad to have found somewhere like home. I filed the location of the club away and tried to keep up with my guide.

The streets were now sluggish with streetcars, bicycles and pedestrians. To my surprise, many of the people we passed were Asian. I also saw a fair number of Indians and Blacks. Mixed couples strolled by, some with babies.

We entered a huge pigeon-filled square intersected by street-cars and surrounded by modern office buildings.

"Where exactly are you from?"

"The coast."

"I mean, are you Dutch?"

"Of course."

"But are your parents Dutch?"

"Yes."

"Both of them?"

That clearly pissed her off. "Yes."

"But you look—"

"Dutch people come in all sizes and colors—exactly as they do in the United States."

I'd hit a nerve, so I decided to come in from a different direction. I glanced at the large church on the other side of the square. A flock of pigeons floated down to the cobblestones beside it.

"You know, this is a very beautiful city."

"Americans always think so."

"Ever been to New York?"

"Yes."

"What did you think?"

"I loved Central Park."

I didn't even bother to answer. All the tourists love the Park. But few of them ever go north of Ninetieth Street. None of them ever brave 110th. They don't know jack about Harlem.

I took a quick glance at Sophie, but she was still looking away. Suddenly I wondered if her answer was meant to be sarcastic.

We approached a stone building fronted by tall Greek columns.

"There you are," Sophie pointed. "The Registry is inside."

She turned to leave and I touched her arm.

"Hey, could you—I mean, do you have time to—"

She looked directly into my eyes. "You'll be fine. I'm sure they'll speak some English."

"Well, I—" again I paused, hoping to hide my insecurity about trying to deal with the Dutch officials alone.

Sophie seemed irritated, as if she was waiting for a child to tie his own shoes. "I think," she said pointedly, "that this is a private matter."

She was right and I knew it. Shit. Of all the times I'd wanted a chick to leave me the hell alone, to respect my privacy and give me some peace, this was one occasion when I really wanted one to stick around.

"Look, I could use your help. You just . . . well, you really seem to know how to take care of business."

She shifted her pack higher up on her shoulder and glanced at her watch. "Okay. I'll come in with you, but I can't stay long. I really have to be somewhere."

We entered the building and Sophie asked a guard for directions. We went down a series of corridors, took a rear elevator, and came out in a long passageway of identical doors. Each one had an official-looking title.

"Perhaps it is a good thing I came," she admitted. "This is more complicated than I expected."

We finally found the Registry—an office with a long counter and rows of records. Sophie spoke to a clerk. Then she turned to me.

"You must fill out a sheet with all the information you know about the person you're seeking. The archivist says it's too late to do the search today, but if you leave the request, they'll search their files tomorrow."

I took one of the printed forms and tried to read it. Sophie again glanced at her watch.

"Sorry, Sophie—I just can't make this out."

She took the paper from my hands. "What is the name of the person you're seeking?"

"I think it's . . ." I took the yellowing scrap of paper from my wallet and unfolded it carefully. Hesitating, I tried to read the smeared letters. "Justina . . . Van . . . Gelder."

Sophie glanced up sharply. "You said you are looking for your mother."

"I am."

"And you don't know her name?"

I looked away, ashamed to admit that I knew almost nothing about her. I had no damn idea what she looked like, where she lived, or what the hell had happened to her after my father took off.

How could I admit to anyone that I was praying that the name I'd found on a scrap of paper inside a filthy jacket when cleaning out Louis's belongings might be hers?

"My father left Amsterdam forty-three years ago. I guess he didn't remember much."

I knew she could hear the humiliation in my voice. She looked at me a moment longer. "I'm sorry. I had no right to be rude."

Soon we were heading out through the maze of corridors. She was speeding up to a near running pace. When we reached the street she turned away. "I must go now. I'm late already."

"Sophie—could we grab a sandwich sometime?"

"Come by Vetiver's if you like."

"Wait—"

She had started to move off and I reached for her, accidentally grasping her arm.

"I—I just wanted to thank you."

"No problem," she snapped, pulling free. And then she was gone.

I stood on the Registry steps. She crossed the street at a run and entered a gray stone building with tall windows. I could see a few other people going inside. It looked like it might be a college.

As I began walking back to my hotel a fine rain began to fall, turning into steam over the subway grills. I smelled something familiar—yeah, a man was making french fries at a sidewalk stand. Up ahead I saw a whole row of greenhouses spilling sun-flowers out onto the street—even though it was December. Coltrane's version of "Greensleeves" started playing in my head as a glassed-in tourist boat, its spotlights shining, floated by on the canal beside me.

Something stirred in my memory and I had a crazy instant of

recognition, as if all of this belonged to me, or as if I truly belonged here. I realized that it was the first time in many years that I didn't want to drink, even though it had been an eternity since I'd known even an hour without my Thirst.

I only wished that Serge was here to share it with me.

I was five days short of my tenth birthday when my grandmother threw up her hands and died in the middle of a storefront church service. Louis's unmarried sister Vanelle, who worked the cash register in a pharmacy, moved in. Vanelle was a tale untold—a woman who trusted her life to romance novels and cheap drugstore perfumes. Tall and bony, she fried chicken wings and okra and didn't have much to say to her brother. After trying to make friends with me for a few weeks—and failing miserably—she had even less to say to me.

Vanelle took the back room and I still slept in the hall, even when I grew so much that my feet pushed against the front door. Louis continued to stagger in from his gigs at dawn, swearing and grumbling as he tripped over me before stumbling to the sofa. I did everything in my power not to wake him up in the mornings—that was when he was his most evil and his belt buckle hurt the worst. Most of the time when I came home from school, he was already gone.

There was no one around to talk to, so I never found a voice for my thoughts. After Louis beat me enough for "getting that 'look' on my face," I learned to hide what I was feeling. Silence protected me from all the shit that could trip me up, both at home and on the streets.

As I grew into manhood I learned to walk with lowered eyes, keeping my limbs tight and my pace cool and steady. I figured that fading into the crowd was the best way to survive.

But Louis's hatred seemed to grow with me.

"What you think you doin'?" he sneered one morning when he caught me in the bathroom, trying to shave. I looked away, embarrassed.

"You like what you see in the mirror, boy?"

I remained silent, the razor shaking in my hand.

"Answer me, punk!"

I said nothing.

"What—you think you a man now?"

When I didn't reply, he shook his head. "Shit. I don't know why you even bothering. You so damn ugly you need to let it grow."

Tears came into my eyes, and my father laughed. "How in the hell did I end up with a punk like you for a son?"

I learned to drink when I was thirteen. Discovering alcohol was more exciting to me than the New World had been to Columbus. I soon quit going to school, preferring to spend my days in alleys, grouped around a bottle with five or six other kids. One day some truant officers hauled us into the principal's office. They called Louis, then waited most of the day before realizing he wasn't going to show up.

So I was sent to an electronics program, where I quickly learned that going to class drunk didn't affect my grades. In fact, a two-dollar pint of hobo fuel made me feel powerful. My walk turned into a glide; my syllables slurred into a kind of hip urban speech, and my lids grew heavy and menacing. Nobody tried to beat my butt anymore.

Now my shyness became a coldness that drove women crazy. I learned about sex in darkened rooms between bottles of malt liquor. When I came home at dawn, filthy from a night on the streets, Vanelle just sucked her teeth and shook her head. "The apple don't fall far," she'd mutter. Louis, still reeling from the weed and booze of the previous night's gig, would stare at me for a moment before rolling over, farting and passing out on the sofa.

I drank my way through the days and nights of my youth. My buddies drank. My women drank, too. I finished the electronics program, but I couldn't keep a job until I started working in the tunnels. And for years my drinking kept me from doing anything more than dragging the heaviest cables into the deepest holes.

I drank when I wasn't working, so bars were my home. I drank when I was fucking, so it didn't matter who I was with. When I was drinking, the mirrors threw back a face that didn't bother me, and neither did my father's silence, or my mother's absence, or any of the other shit that made up my life.

In fact, there was nothing like that moment when that first drink of the day hit my system.

I fucking loved being a drunk.

I gave twenty years of my life to the bottle.

It took me twenty damn years to understand that even if I loved the bottle, the bottle didn't give a shit about me. It just loved controlling me. And loving that bottle wasn't giving me any kind of protection from the people who had fucked up my life.

Which is one reason I didn't know how to deal with the idea that anyone would want to help me fight my Thirst. Even when I got desperate, I refused to ask anybody for help. I knew all about the meetings and the programs—hell, plenty of guys down in the tunnels were on the wagon. But I just knew that none of them was going through the same shit as me.

And then I finally hit my bottom and staggered into my first meeting. I don't remember too much about that night. But I do remember this cat sitting down next to me, holding out his hand and introducing himself as Serge Kovel. I didn't know it at that time, but Serge was throwing me the line that would save my life.

Now, it's true that Serge was white. But he wasn't white like the white cats that march up and down Fifth Avenue carrying a briefcase. Serge was the kind of white that grew up with parents straight off the boat from the Ukraine, in an apartment surrounded by former residents of San Juan. "I'm Puerto-Krainian," he liked to say.

Serge made his living as a seventh-grade social studies teacher, taking the train in from Brooklyn and staying late every evening to attend meetings. At five foot five, with slick black hair, he didn't know how to be a cold-blooded Anglo-Saxon shark. He even liked jazz.

Truth was, Serge had been so busy struggling to get over his family's Old World mentality that he never had the time to learn how to be a bigot. I'd never met anyone who was so willing to discuss America's obsession with race.

"It's about mind fucking," he said during our first meal together, in his favorite diner over on West Fourteenth. "The Founding Fathers realized they had to unite all the European immigrants behind the idea of being white. That way they wouldn't side with Blacks. After all, Thomas Jefferson and George Washington needed those African people to run their plantations."

"What the hell are you talking about? That has nothing to do with the way white people behave today."

"Of course it does. White men have had all the money and power since this country began. Every immigrant who comes here figures out pretty damn fast which race he wants to belong to."

"Including your parents?"

"Shit. My parents didn't even know what *white* was until they got to America. They were just a couple of peasants who got caught in the crossfire between the Nazis and the Communists."

"They still got more power in this country than Black people."

"Oh, hell, Abe! My father had to Americanize his name just to get a job collecting garbage, and my mother never even learned to speak English. They spent their lives eating potatoes and cabbage and being glad as hell that they weren't starving to death in the mother country."

"So why do you like hanging out with Black people?"

"That's because of this beautiful Trinidadian girl I fell in love with in the sixth grade. I never got to tell her because her big brother Reginald saw me grinning at her one day and chased me home with a baseball bat."

We both laughed, but a part of me wasn't buying it.

"Look, Abe," he said to me during our second meal together, "addiction is one way the rich folks stay in power in this country. They may sip some century-old Bordeaux, but they leave the dollar-a-pint bourbon for you and me. While they're relaxing after a hard day on Wall Street with some Cristal champagne, we're capping off our hustle with malt liquor and a crack pipe. They make it cheap and easy for us to destroy both our brains and our guts."

"What are you—some kind of conspiracy freak?"

"No. I've just watched too many brothers and sisters from the working classes lose their lives by ingesting poison."

"So when did you start drinking?"

"I was already drinking at nine," he said with a shrug. "And I wasn't stealing the church wine, like the other altar boys. I started out with the schnapps my father distilled in our cellar, like all the men did in the Old Country. The shit wasn't even ripe, but it got me high and there was plenty of it."

"Your father didn't miss it?"

"Are you kidding? He thought it was funny. He told my mother that boys with strong *juices* like to drink. He said it would make a man out of me." Serge burst into laughter. "My dad was drinking so much himself that he couldn't even see that booze was turning us both into morons."

"Is he still drinking?"

"Naw. They cut most of his liver out last year. Now he gets off on painkillers."

"So why did you quit?"

"I quit because I saw what it did to my first marriage. I really loved Cecilia, but I was busy fucking every other woman I could. Seemed like the more I cheated, the more I drank. And when I drank it was easy to cheat. I finally ended up in rehab, and after I got out she wasn't willing to take any more chances on me. I spent a couple of years getting myself together, and now I'm with Angie." He placed his left hand on the table to show me his wedding ring. "There really is a brave new world waiting for those who have the guts to quit."

"Guts?"

"Yeah, man. A drunk is nothing but an escape artist. He uses the bottle to hide from all the pressures of life. But the fact that you had the guts to seek help with your drinking—well, Abe, that already took extreme courage. I'm proud of you. And I promise you that if you're willing to put it in the hands of your Higher Power, your life can start making sense again."

It took me a long time to get comfortable with Serge Kovel. Comfortable with the idea that he could care about me. He was, quite possibly, the only person besides my grandmother who had ever really cared if I was dead or alive.

One night, about nine months after we met, I asked him again why he was always there for me.

"Look, the only person who really understands this shit is another addict. The only person who can really help is a clean addict."

"But what are you getting out of this?"

"This is when you know you're winning the struggle, Abe. It's not when you can comfortably refuse the beer at the family barbeque, or stroll past your favorite corner bar without stopping. It's when you're finally ready to do your best to help someone else. Not necessarily the person you're in love with, either. I mean, it's a willingness to be there for any damn body who needs it. A friend or a neighbor, or even some cable-lugging, tunnel-dwelling Harlemite, like you."

"So that's why you're always hanging around."

"I'm here, Abel, because I see somebody real cool deep down inside of you and I want to help you find him."

"Why?"

"Because," Serge said with a smile, "I'm really going to like being his friend."

I can handle the nights as long as I'm working. It's the weekends and holidays that kick my ass. And that first night in Amsterdam looked like it might just fuck me up. So after walking back and forth in my room like a caged animal for what seemed like hours, I threw on my jacket and took the elevator down to the lobby.

The guy behind the desk jumped to his feet.

"Good evening, sir."

"Evening."

"Are you planning to dine in our restaurant?"

"Not tonight."

"May I offer you a list of restaurants in the area?"

"I'm fine."

"Shall I call you a taxi, sir?"

"No, thanks."

"Would you like a map of the city?"

"I think I can find my way around."

"May I assist you in any other way?"

"I'm all right," I said as I backed toward the entrance.

"Very good, sir," he called behind me. "I must remind you that the exterior doors will be locked at eleven, and then you must use your room key to enter the hotel. The night concierge will be on duty after that time. Have a nice evening."

Sweet Jesus, I thought as I finally made it outside. You need to cut down on the caffeine.

The night air was cool and damp and smelled of car exhaust and standing water. A bicycle glided by, its wheels wet with rainwater. Christmas lights were shining at the end of the block. Since I didn't know where the hell I was going, I began walking in that direction.

Now, I'd been working nights for twenty-five years. I was used to watching the sun rise as I went to sleep. And I was often on my way down the shaft of a tunnel as the sun set. I guess I never really fit in with people who take care of their shit during the day.

All I know is that the minute I hit the nighttime streets, Amsterdam began making sense to me. It wasn't just the network of canals and bridges, which reminded me of the grid of tunnels where I spent my life. I was actually starting to feel the vibe of the place.

"They got joints in Amsterdam that serve beer all day and all night, too," my father used to say when I was a kid. "Brown beer and red beer and white beer and beer sweetened with honey. And the beer over there don't make you sick like the piss they got in the bars here."

I remember staring at him in disbelief, imagining clear glasses of foaming vanilla or strawberry alcohol, tasting like ice cream and pouring from crystal taps.

"The folks over there put liquor in everything," my father

continued. "They even fry pancakes on the street and flavor 'em with booze.

"And they got stores where you can walk in and buy all the weed you can smoke. You can sit right down and light up with your buddies, and the law don't say nothin'. People over there understand there ain't no harm done by getting high."

That sounded like some bullshit. By then some of my classmates had already been hauled down to the precinct for trying to sell weed. Could the police in Amsterdam really be down with the drug trade?

"And after you get your buzz on you can go window shopping for some pussy!" Louis said when I was fourteen. "That's right—they got the bitches sitting right behind these big panes of glass. You just walk along the street, decide what you like, knock on the door, and she closes the shades and goes to work—"

"Naw, Pop!" I protested, certain that all those years of drinking had finally sent my father's brain down the toilet. "That's crazy!"

"No it ain't. They got ho's from all over the world for a man to choose from. It's completely legal and don't nobody care."

"I don't *even* believe that!"

"Don't matter if you believe me. It's the goddamn truth!"

No, Pop, it's not, I thought as I made my way through Amsterdam's dark streets. This place is about a whole lot more than your liquor-soaked mind could deal with.

In some ways, the city reminded me of the West Village, with its rows of town houses and narrow streets. But Manhattan was like Dizzy Gillespie—moving at a pace and rhythm that nearly took your breath away. This place was more like Monk. A moodiness hung over those steep roofs and the low December sky.

My mind leapt to the congested avenues that moved thousands of vehicles through the center of Manhattan. I thought of the walls of traffic that roared between stoplights, ready to crush anyone stupid enough to get in the way. Amsterdam, on the other hand, was full of bicycles, and even late in the night folks were rolling along, going about their lives.

I leaned over a railing to peer into a canal. Leaves drifted by in the black water. Damn, I thought, don't people fall in? Slip on the ice or some shit like that? Get drunk and take a surprise splash?

I chuckled at the vision of myself, back in the day, staggering home from Sugar's Bar and ending up twelve feet under. I sure as hell didn't know how to swim. That would be one hell of a way to commit murder: just invite your enemy for a few drinks, then give him a hug and a shove.

I wandered on, looking down streets that were way too narrow for America's hogs. The cars in Amsterdam were like little shoeboxes lined up along the scrubbed white curbs.

Then I looked up at the houses, rising four or five stories to steep roofs. "Will you look at that," I whispered. "These folks don't even bother to close their drapes at night!"

There were two young couples at a table, drinking wine and eating spaghetti. They were talking and laughing together.

I stopped in the shadows, watching. I had never been to a formal dinner party in somebody's home. Nee Cee refused to cook and none of her friends were in relationships. She liked to drag me around to parties where everybody drank gin and ate wings standing up. The guests had to yell to be heard over the music, and Nee Cee would go crazy if I so much as made eye contact with another sister.

What would it be like to spend an evening in someone's home, having a meal and a quiet conversation? With some

Kenny Barron playing in the background. Then maybe taking a taxi over to a jazz club. Coming home late to make slow love. Maybe even with someone I really dug?

Through another window I saw a woman on a bed in her bathrobe, painting her toenails in the light of the TV. I turned quickly away, a nervous prickling sensation racing down my spine. What the hell was I thinking? What if a cop had seen me looking at her?

Still, I found myself watching an old couple sitting on a sofa, the woman knitting while the man held a beer mug. It was hard to believe that anybody could stay together long enough to look like that.

I passed corner stores with crazy shit in the windows: an Eiffel Tower and an Empire State Building carved from white chocolate, with some little fudge trees, cars, and candy people strolling along below. Florists with bizarre-looking cactuses under violet lights. Antique shops with everything from oil paintings to women's corsets.

And everywhere I turned I saw diamond merchants.

This was crazy different from home, where street vendors sold their art, music, oils, and homemade health remedies on colorful stands. Harlem was full of brothers and sisters trying to make it on mother wit and guts. Poor folks will sell anything they got, and convince you to like it, too.

But this place was all about money. Travel agents were advertising tours to the Seychelles, Cape Verde, Mauritius—*and where the hell was that?* Stores were even selling Oriental rugs larger than my fucking apartment.

Somebody's making *too* much money here, I thought. Louis must have been crazy to walk away from this and practically starve to death in the Sta—

I came to a full stop outside a bright window stocked with

my idea of heaven and hell: bottles of wine. Beers with bright labels. Honeyed cognacs, dark brandies and pale vermouths. Twelve-year-old Scottish single malts. Caramel-flavored rums. Wood-cured Russian vodkas.

My Thirst rushed to my head as if I had stood up too fast.

Serge, I thought, almost tumbling over a bicycle parked next to the shop's entrance. You *really* need to see this!

Just keep it moving, Abe, his voice answered, and I forced myself to turn away.

It was late when I chanced on the streets where Black and white and yellow women sat in the windows, red lights glowing over their tight little G-strings and cutaway bras.

So Louis had got this one thing right, I thought, staring into a picture window where two Asian women in silvery bikinis massaged cream onto each other's shoulders. Their black hair was pinned up so that a few strands fell over their faces. They looked out at me with come-and-get-it smiles.

A metallic taste flooded my mouth as the smaller woman winked with thick eyelashes. I reached inside my pocket and clasped my money roll with sweating fingers. Yeah, I know: I didn't come to Amsterdam to do any shit like this. But those bitches were looking too damn good and Nee Cee was too damn far away to matter.

Just as I started for the door I heard a hometown voice.

"Sorry, my brother, but we got an appointment!"

Two brothers in American army uniforms pushed by me and rang the doorbell. One of them looked at me and smiled. The door clicked open and they went inside. A venetian blind slid down over the window.

I stood there for a moment, feeling like a fool. Then I decided it didn't matter. Cats living with other cats in barracks needed some pussy more urgently than I did.

I wandered back toward the Rembrandtsplein, where I'd heard the saxophone earlier that evening. Groups of people stood around the club entrance, talking and laughing together. Cigarette smoke was trapped on the humid air and I felt like I was back in Harlem.

As I got closer several people noticed me and started muttering to each other. Three or four others turned around to look, so I pulled up the collar of my jacket and kept on walking. I didn't know what that shit meant, but it was late and as my grandmother would have said, I was a stranger in a very strange land.

It was near dawn when I returned to the hotel. I had finally figured it out: Amsterdam was Stan Getz playing with Bill Evans. Most of the night had sounded cool and bittersweet, just like the two of them performing "Grandfather's Waltz."

Lying down on the bed in my clothes, I stared at the ceiling, thankful that I'd made it sober through my first twenty-four hours in Amsterdam.

"A man and his mama."

"What did you say?" I paused, the razor poised just at the tip of my chin. Hugh Masekela was playing in the background—I always counted on the African brothers to help me out when I was trying to let go of a particularly bad night.

Nee Cee was leaning in the doorway, her bleached hair looking harsh against her brown skin. Her full breasts were pressed tight against the fabric of one of my T-shirts. She was slapping her open palm with my plane ticket and staring at me with those rattlesnake eyes.

"I said—a man and his mama."

I slowly lowered the blade. "Meaning?"

"I don't know what in hell you trying to find over there."

"I don't think it's any of your goddamn business."

"Of course it's my business. You spending time and money that could be used for better things."

"Such as?"

"For one, you don't need to be living in a dump like this. You a workingman with a paycheck."

"So I got to spend it just because I earn it?"

"You could move in with me and save even more, if that's what you call yourself doing."

"I like living in Harlem."

"You could get a bigger place in Queens."

"My job is here."

"You could take the train, like millions of people."

"I don't like trains."

"You don't like nothing."

"I like things the way they are."

Once again I lifted my razor to my face. Nee Cee shifted her weight to her other leg and sucked her teeth.

"So why you going to Amsterdam?"

"You know why."

"How long do you intend to be over there?"

"A couple of weeks."

"What you think you gonna find? Your mother is probably dead. Or she moved away. Or got together with some white guy and don't want to see your Black face at her door."

I stared at the reflection of my Black face. Suddenly my hand was trembling. "Shut up, woman," I whispered, suspending the sharp razor above my waiting flesh.

"You need to listen to somebody other than Serge. I don't know why you trust that white man anyway."

"He don't waste time talking shit, like you."

"Talk about wasting time? The only thing you do is work and go to those stupid meetings—"

"My meetings keep me alive, Nee Cee."

"That's bullshit. You ain't had a drink since I've known you."

"That's because of my meetings."

"You know what I think? You're addicted to your addiction, Abel. That's why you can't move out of this place or get a better job or hook up with a woman. The only thing you can think about is your goddamn meetings and your fellow former drunk, Serge Whiteman Kovel."

"You need to shut up, woman."

"You don't feel nothin' and you don't do nothin' for nobody but yourself."

"Then you can get the fuck out of here."

"You want me to leave you alone, Abel? Because that's what you'll be—sitting up in this dump all by yourself. You and your buddy Serge."

"Fuck you, bitch." I set down the razor and grasped the edge of the sink. Nee Cee's head snapped from side to side as she moved closer, raising a finger to my face.

"You need to face it, Abel. I'm all you got in this world and it's time you showed me some respect. You need to get your shit together and stop living in a fantasy about some white woman who probably can't even remember your name!"

I don't remember when my right hand came off the sink. I was only glad that I was able to stop myself before Louis took over and beat the shit out of her. Instead, I took her by the arm and walked her to the bathroom door.

"I told you to get the fuck out."

She looked up at me and smiled. "That's all right, Abel. But you think about this when you're by yourself over there wishing you had somebody looking out for you. Because your white boy's gonna be a long way away and there won't be any goddamn meetings for you to go to."

I woke up from a shitty dream. I was having sex with Nee Cee, but every time I looked at her she had a different face.

The hotel room was flooded with cold gray light. My back hurt. My legs hurt and my head hurt. The air was sour with smoke from the overloaded ashtray and the sheets were damp with sweat.

"Good morning, asshole," I murmured. It was already noon.

I laid there for a long time, trying to get my head together. I needed some food. I wanted to drink.

You listen to me, I thought, like Serge taught me to do. You are forty-fucking-five years old. You've survived being Black and male and poor. You've survived twenty-five years in the tunnels. You survived that motherfucker Louis Crofton. And you are surviving your Thirst. You will not give up now.

The trip back to the Registry took fucking forever. Either I had been paying too much attention to Sophie's ass the night before, or while I was sleeping they had done something shitty with the streets. I mean, Amsterdam may look like parts of lower Manhattan, but they sure as hell hadn't hired the same city planner. Whereas New York is laid out in a way that makes sense—Forty-third Street is one block north of Forty-second—the streets in Amsterdam were all Ornette Coleman, with twists and turns that always seemed to lead me back to the same fucking canal. Or maybe it was a different fucking canal that looked just the same as the one before.

I searched for the giant square I'd crossed with Sophie, but it had vanished in a mess of bicycles and pedestrians. Finding myself trapped in an area with streets as narrow as alleys, I wandered helplessly as Christmas shoppers rushed like rabbits between the stores.

The smell of fresh bread and warm beer drifted from sandwich shops, but my tense stomach wasn't about to let me eat. Vendors were frying thin pancakes on a street-side griddle, flavoring them with butter, sugar, whipped cream and—*shit, Louis was right about that, too*—liquor. For a moment I stopped, wishing with all my heart that I could eat one soaked in Grand Marnier.

Eventually I found my way to the big-pillared building. The Registry's doors were propped open. I nodded at the clerk behind the counter, who immediately came forward to greet me.

"Oh, hello Mr. Crofton." The clerk, a middle-aged woman in bifocals, seemed genuinely happy. "I have good news for you."

I put my hands in my pockets, hoping she wouldn't notice that they were shaking. She pushed a single sheet of paper toward me and smiled up through her thick lenses.

"Our records indicate that a Justina Maria Van Gelder was born on December 24, 1934. Is this birth date correct?"

"I—I don't know."

"But this is the correct name?"

"I think so."

She bent her head and ran her finger along the paper. "Mrs. Van Gelder worked in this city from 1966 until 1999. She probably took her retirement at that time."

"Is she—" I swallowed—"is she still living?"

"There is no record of her death," the woman said gently.

I leaned over the counter, trying to decipher the document. "Do you know where she lives now?"

"The records indicate that all her files were sent to Haarlem."

"*Harlem?*" The word crashed against me like a sledgehammer. "You mean she went to live in America?"

"America?"

"Harlem. You know—Harlem in New York?"

"Not New York. Haarlem is in the Netherlands."

"There's a place called Harlem in the Netherlands?"

"Yes—just outside Amsterdam. You can go with the bus or train," she said, nodding.

I stared at her stupidly. Then a thought wormed its way up from my years at P.S. 182: *Of course there could be a Harlem here. New York was fucking founded by the Dutch!*

"Do you—do you have an address for her?"

The clerk shook her head. "You must take this paper to the Registry in Haarlem, unless of course she is listed by chance in the telephone book."

I pulled my money out and handed the woman a bill. She again shook her head. "No, sir. This is my job."

"Please," I said, pressing the bill into her hand. "Please take it. Please."

She pushed the money back to me and smiled. "Good luck, Mr. Crofton."

Soon I was standing on the street. My heart was banging so hard that I could barely hear the rattling streetcars and hundreds of people walking around me. Staring into the crowd I had just one thought: *I need to talk to Serge about this*—but he was on the other side of the world, and I wasn't about to share this with Nee Cee. The only other person I could talk to was Sophie.

Making my way back as fast as I could—I had no idea which damn streetcar to take—I eventually stumbled on the canal that faced Café Vetiver. But instead of finding Sophie behind the counter, I came face-to-face with a tall blonde with pale skin and ice blue eyes.

She glanced up from the wine she was pouring and checked me out fast. Her eyes changed and she greeted me in a low voice.

"I don't speak Dutch."

"Ah—American. So what can I do for you?"

"I was looking for Sophie."

"Sophie?" The waitress raised an eyebrow. "She's not here."

"Can you tell me how to find her?"

The woman's smile went dry. She set the wineglass on a napkin and came out from behind the counter to serve a customer. I knew she was giving me a chance to reconsider. When she returned she leaned toward me, her face inches from mine.

"Sophie doesn't like to be found on her day off."

"She can tell me that."

"I'm a lot more fun."

"I'm not looking for fun."

She paused, her eyes licking my face. Then she shrugged.

"Third house on the left. Ring the top flat. And remember," she said as she pushed hair from her eyes, "you're welcome to come back anytime."

I found the house, a four-story building covered with ivy facing the canal, and rang the bell. After a long moment someone answered. I spoke into the intercom and a buzzer sounded. The marble foyer was filled with cool light and I hesitated for a moment, knowing my Black ass didn't belong there. Still, I made my way to the top landing and knocked on the door. Somebody looked through a bronze peephole, and the door swung open.

A white-haired man of about my height stood on the threshold, a newspaper in one hand. He was dressed completely in black, like some goddamn mortician.

"Excuse me—I'm looking for Sophie."

Dr. Doom took his time examining my clothes. Then he stared into my face with hard gray eyes. "Who are you?"

"Elias—" we both heard Sophie's voice as she approached from inside the apartment. She said something in Dutch and the man moved aside very slowly, still blocking the doorway. Sophie appeared next to him in a short white bathrobe, her wild curls dripping.

"Abel—what are you doing here?"

"I . . . I just wanted to talk to you."

"Who told you where I live?"

"The woman working in the café."

"I see." She paused a moment and the man rustled his newspaper noisily. Sophie ignored him.

"You returned to the Registry?"

"Yes. The clerk said that my mother worked here until a few years ago. Now she might be in Haarlem, and I—I just dropped by to thank you for your help."

Sophie explained something to her companion in Dutch. He exhaled loudly and vanished into the crib.

She came out onto the stairwell and closed the door softly behind her. "What will you do now?"

"I guess I'm on my way to Haarlem. I grew up in Harlem, you know. The *real* Harlem."

She gave me a dry smile. "*Tot ziens*, Abel. I hope it goes well for you."

I knew she was really just telling me to get lost. But for some reason I still stood there, pretending I didn't understand. Maybe it was that bet I had made with myself the day before.

"I was wondering if—well, maybe you could show me some more of the city sometime."

Sophie lowered her dark eyes. "I am very busy."

"I could drop by this evening, when you get off work."

"I'm not working today."

"What about tomorrow?"

"Why don't you speak to Galine, at the café?"

"I'd rather speak to you."

She glanced up. Our eyes met and I reached for her hand. She moved away, avoiding my touch.

"Hey," I said quickly. "I'm not trying to—"

"Good-bye, Abel. And good luck."

"And why do you think you need to find her?"

I was walking with Serge a few days before I got on the plane for Amsterdam. We were leaving a meeting and the early winter wind was kicking New York's ass.

"Because I don't know a damn thing about her."

"Maybe you don't want to know," he replied as he flicked a lighter up to a Kool.

"Or maybe my father just didn't want me to." I pulled my collar up against the blast that roared out from between the buildings.

Serge pocketed his lighter and drew hard on the cigarette. His green eyes narrowed to watery squints as the wind blew the smoke into his face. "Your old man wouldn't even tell you her name?"

"Took it with him to his grave."

"There might be a reason—"

"Sure there's a reason. Louis Crofton was a mean motherfucking son of a bitch."

We both laughed, though we knew it wasn't funny. We made our way along the cracked sidewalk, shoulders bent against the cold. I caught our reflection in a store window: a tall black man and a short white man cracking bad jokes about my life's stupid reality show.

"You're not scared to fly?" Serge asked, nodding down the avenue toward the void where the Twin Towers used to be.

"I'm afraid to fly sober," I answered, avoiding his eyes.

"Hang on." He stopped to take my arm. "If you're not ready to make this trip you should put it off for a few months. In fact, if you wait until summer I'll come with you."

"I don't want to wait," I replied, shifting inside my insulated jacket. "I've been putting this off my whole fucking life. Come on, Serge—it's no big thing. All I have to do is get on the bird, sleep for six hours, and when I wake up I'm in Holland."

"But how are you going to get around? You don't speak the language."

"They got lots of Americans over there. And people from England, too. Louis told me once that he never needed to learn a word of Dutch, or Hollandaise, or whatever it is they speak."

"Big surprise," Serge remarked, a stream of smoke coming out of his mouth as well. "The only language your daddy ever spoke was bottlese."

I grunted in agreement. We crossed the rush-hour street, jogging the last few steps to avoid a rush of oncoming cars.

"You know, family shit can really fuck up your sobriety," he said as we started up Broadway.

"Sometimes I think that finding my mother is the only thing that'll keep me sober."

Flicking his cigarette into the gutter, Serge reached up to clap my shoulder. "In the long run, knowing will hurt less than not knowing. You'll be all right, buddy. Take your book of meditations along and do your daily readings. Try to hook up with a group over there for a little support."

"I'll be looking for a hookup, all right!" I laughed, but Serge stayed serious.

"Look, Abe, I've known you for how long? Twelve years, right? We've seen each other through some pretty fucked up shit. You made me see reason when I was about to screw things up with Angie. And I want you to understand that you don't have to pretend with me."

"What do you mean?"

"I mean, brother, that if I was you I'd be scared shitless. You're talking about getting on a plane and flying off to a different country, where they don't speak English, to try to find a woman who may not even be alive. Who may not have told anybody that she has a son in America. A Black son, at that."

I looked down, scraping the asphalt with the steel toe of my work boots. "All I really want to do is see her, Serge. Just get a look at her. I want to see the woman who made a child with Louis Crofton. The woman who put up with his shit for years—"

"Maybe—" Serge spat on the sidewalk—"he only stayed with her because he didn't want to come back here."

"You're probably right. He never quit complaining about how much he hated New York. Sometimes I think the only reason he got on that plane was because his mother and sister were here."

"But your father didn't give a shit about your family."

"I was a different thing."

"Meaning?"

"He put me in my grandmother's hands for a reason. I think that every time he looked at me, he was seeing my mother— whoever she was. I think he brought me back here because he was determined to make a Crofton out of me."

"You mean, because your mother was white?"

"Maybe. Or maybe not."

"I don't get it."

"Neither do I." I inhaled slowly. "That's why I've got to go."

"Listen," Serge said quietly, "you're gonna be by yourself over there. And you really won't know who to trust—"

"I don't trust anybody here, except you."

"That's what I'm trying to say. I want you to call me any-time—night or day—if you need anything."

Serge pulled me close in a rough embrace, then pushed me away and raised one eyebrow. "Before you get on that plane you've got to get some new rags, my friend."

I looked down at my insulated overalls and scuffed boots. "Don't think my mama will want to own her working-class son?"

"It's those greaseballs at immigration I'm worried about. If you turn up at the airport wearing this shit they might take you for a terrorist. And one other thing—" he looked into my eyes. "You got to clean up your act and talk like you've got some edu-cation when you get there."

"You mean I can't show them my true self?"

"That's something neither one of us can ever afford to do."

We both chuckled for a moment, then together watched a high-heeled Dominicana strut by.

"And if you see something pretty," Serge added shaking his head, "do me a favor and get some for me."

The trip to Haarlem was short—less than half an hour, twenty-five minutes at most. The train cut a straight path across the flattest land I'd ever seen. In the distance I could make out some little stone houses, cranking windmills, and the occasional solitary tree.

As the train began to slow down I let out a whistle. Like Amsterdam, the city of Haarlem was built on a series of canals ringing out from the town center. Many of the houses looked real old, and even the newer ones were built with the same plain brown bricks.

I walked out of the train station and into a kind of Dutch Disneyland. Everything was too clean, too orderly and too damn quiet. The streets were full of people—I mean, it didn't look too different from Amsterdam in that regard—but there was this small-town vibe of no fear, no hate, no goddamn thing to worry about.

And one other thing stuck out: There wasn't a Black face to be found.

That shit made me nervous.

I began my hunt for the town center. I followed a busy thoroughfare three or four short blocks until it opened onto a wide stone square surrounded by cafés, tourist shops and a church with a couple of tall towers.

"Hello, mister!"

I turned around to face a teenager with the faded blond hair and gray eyes that I saw on many of the Dutch. The kid was carrying a backpack and wore a short ponytail like the white boys in rock videos.

He was standing a few feet away, but he came a step closer. He couldn't have been more than sixteen or seventeen years old.

"You are from America?"

"Ah—yeah."

"My name's Matthias."

"What?"

"*Mat-ee-ahs*. I learn English at school. Sometimes during my free hour I come here to talk to the tourists. It's nice to practice English a bit with someone."

I managed a smile. He began talking faster.

"You are here for the Christmas holiday?"

"Something like that."

"You need a place to stay?"

"No thanks. I'm all set."

"You are hungry?"

I gestured toward the cafés. "Looks like there's plenty to eat."

"You are perhaps from Los Angeles?"

"No. New York."

"I see. You have big towers there—I believe you call them 'sky-cutters'?"

"Skyscrapers."

"That's right. I want very much to go to America one day."

"I hope you'll get to do that."

Fastening his gaze on the sidewalk, the kid looked like he

was struggling to find something else to say. Finally he gave up and held out his hand. "Welcome to Haarlem!"

I looked into his pimply young face and felt myself smile. Then I chuckled, and the chuckle grew into a laugh. The kid burst into embarrassed laughter, too.

"I am sorry I do not know what to say."

"You're doing just fine, Matthias. You can call me Abel."

"Ah! Like the Bible?"

"That's it. Look, Matthias, since you want to speak some English—can you tell me where to find a phone?"

"Oh, yes! You can call America from the post office." He pointed enthusiastically. "It's right over there."

"I don't want to call the States. I'm looking for someone here in Haarlem."

"Someone in my city?"

"Yes." I decided to take a chance. "A woman named Justina Van Gelder."

He squinted, working his way through my jacked-up pronunciation of the Dutch name. "Sorry," he finally said with a shrug. "You can call for information. There are English-speaking operators. Or I could translate."

"I'll be all right. And Matthias"—he grinned at my accent— "is there a Family Registry here in Haarlem?"

"Registry?"

"The building where you keep the records of births and deaths."

"Ah, the Bevolkings Register. This building is just there, on the other side of the big church."

"Thanks," I said. We shook hands and I patted him on the shoulder.

"I hope," he said proudly, "that you enjoy your visit to my city."

Inside the quiet post office I found the telephone books beside a phone booth along the back wall. The Haarlem directory had at least five fuckin' pages of Van Gelders—but no Justina.

I dug in my pockets for loose change and closeted myself in a booth. Pumping money into the phone, I pressed 0 and waited. A Dutch voice responded, and I asked for someone who could speak English.

A few moments later I exited the tiny cell.

Dead end. The operator had no listing for my mother.

Easy does it, I thought. Just stay cool and see what's going on at the Registry.

A half hour later I was back on the street. I unfolded a small map and stared at it, trying to get my orientation despite the fact that my hands were shaking.

The clerk had found the records in no time.

"Justina Van Gelder's house is number twenty-nine on the Laurier Weg."

"The Laurier *what?*"

She pulled the small map from beneath the counter and penciled the directions in red. "The Laurier Weg is here. Do you see? Six blocks away, across these four canals. It is just after the market district."

"Do I need to take a taxi?"

"A taxi? No. You can walk there in perhaps fifteen minutes."

Forcing myself to breathe slowly, I began moving like a robot through the town. I passed the shops and florists and food vendors. I saw the storefronts change into private houses. Unlocked bicycles were leaning beside the wooden doors. Housewives looked up from their scrubbing as I passed their kitchens.

Then I was crossing the last of the bridges, which stretched over a canal filled with houseboats.

I was standing at the entrance of the Laurier Weg.

But it didn't look like the rest of Haarlem.

First of all, it was nothing more than a narrow, dark alley. The houses were lined up on both sides so that all the doors and windows were parallel. Every door was painted black, and the only sign of life was a patch of ivy trying to grow along the damp bricks.

I started walking real slow, visible to anyone looking out from the windows. Squinting at the numbers on the identical doors, I stopped at number 29, roughly at the center of the block.

Should I ring or knock? Would she see a Black stranger on her doorstep and be afraid to answer?

I raised my hand. I grasped the brass knocker and let it drop. A hollow sound echoed through the house. I waited, listening for some sign of life.

At first there was nothing. Then I heard movement. My stomach contracted and my breath went cold as the door groaned and rolled open.

A pale young woman, her jet-black bangs nearly hiding the two silver rings poked through her left eyebrow, stared at me. A cigarette was stuck between her black-lined lips.

"Ah—is this the Van Gelder house?"

She cocked her head. "No."

"Do you know the Van Gelders?"

"No."

"But this is the address—"

"Wait," she said through a yawn. Her tongue was pierced, too. "I rent only the lower flat."

"Who lives upstairs?"

"No one. You want to rent it?"

"No. I am looking for the owner."

She shrugged. "I don't know who owns the house. I rent from a—how do you say in English? An agency."

My heart crashed. The woman leaned in the doorway, squinting through the cigarette smoke.

"Well—can you tell me the name of the agency?"

"Wait." She disappeared into the house. I stared at the brick wall until she came back, a paper in her hand.

"Ajax," she said simply, pronouncing the word as *Eye-yaks.* She tore off the top of the page. "You take this. Agency address and telephone."

I looked at the paper. "How do I get there?"

She pursed her black lips, then pointed back toward town. "Go to the big square. Near the tall church. But—" she raised her arm to look at a neon watch. "But now it is too late, I think. Perhaps tomorrow."

Thanking her, I took the slip of paper and put it in my pocket. She nodded once and closed the door and I stood in the center of the alley, trying to get my head together.

"You need to put it in the hands of your Higher Power," Serge started telling me when I first got clean.

"Come on, brother. You know I don't believe in your white man's god."

"It doesn't have to be like that. You can think of your Higher Power as the people you love and the people who love you."

"That won't work. I don't know anybody who fits into either category."

"Then make up a god for yourself. Make him black or blue or yellow or any color you want. Make Him a Her. Or an *It,* for that matter."

"What's the point if I have to make it up?"

"The point is that you have to give up control, Abe. Admit that you can't do it alone. Admit that you need help from somebody else."

"So that god can make me feel better?"

"So that God can keep your life on the road when you hit a patch of ice."

"Let's get real, Serge. Where was god when my grandmother was growing up in a sharecropper's shack?"

"God was giving her the courage to go on."

"Where was god when we practically starved in those two freezing rooms on 138th?"

"You're still here, Abe."

"Where was god when my father was beating the shit out of me?"

"He gave you the strength to endure."

"And where the fuck was god when I took my first drink?"

"Ask Him," Serge said. "Ask God why all that shit went down."

"You mean, ask him to explain why he wasn't there?"

"Ask Him how you survived to ask Him about it."

"That's too damn many questions, Serge. I'll be dead before I have time to hear all the answers."

"You may not believe me, but talking to God really can help."

"That's some bullshit, Serge. I made it this far without him. I'm not giving in now."

My Thirst was real bad that night.

Probably because I had come so damn close, but I was still so far away.

Haarlem had been nothing but dead ends. What was worse, the dead ends all sounded like Miles. Lonely Miles. Down-on-his-luck Miles. The echoing-midnight, soul-wrenching Miles whose horn made you feel like you were the last person left in the world.

The girl was right: the Ajax agency was closed when I got there. A sign on the door said the office was open from nine to three. I would have to wait until the following morning to contact them. And then, as I stood there like a fool, an icy rain started falling and I ran all the way back to the train station with Miles's trumpet moaning in my head.

When my train pulled into Amsterdam the rush hour was raging. I had to make my way through crowds of people trying to get out of the rain. Shitty music with sleigh bells and sickly sweet voices blasted out of stores. Folks were lined up to get into restaurants and the café terraces were packed.

It took me a long time to find my way home. At one point I looked up and saw that giant Heineken sign grinning down at me. When I finally stumbled on the hotel, I skipped the slow-moving elevator and climbed all five flights of stairs to my room.

I'm in fucking exile, I thought as I laid on the bed, listening to the sounds echoing up from the street below. I need to go downstairs, sit in a bar and have a couple of gin and tonics with a nice Dutch girl, then bring her back to this room and fuck her brains out.

Sobriety was fucking exile.

My Thirst never died.

I stared at my watch. I couldn't believe that it was only nine o'clock.

The pocket-sized book of meditations, my bon-voyage gift from Serge, was lying on the bedside table. I needed to call him,

but it was just after three in New York. Serge would still be at
school.

Well, god, I thought. Serge has been telling me for years that
I should get to know you. Are you willing to keep me company
tonight?

I listened for a moment as if I really expected to hear an
answer.

No, I guess you're busy with some righteous motherfucker.
Not a prayer-deficient, nonbelieving drunk, like me.

I pushed my feet into my shoes and slowly stood up.

Outside the rain had stopped, leaving a thin fog. The cobble-
stone courtyard of the Rembrandtsplein was now full of people
passing around bottles of beer beneath the dripping trees. I turned
away from the lights and the noise, moving toward darker passages
that felt more like home.

Soon I made my way into a knot of alleys lined with Thai
food stands and sausage grills. A pastry shop smelled like fresh
butter and sugared waffles. I walked over to the display case and
saw something that stopped me cold: a tray of chocolate faces,
the hair made of coconut, the bulging eyes and thick lips drawn
on with white and scarlet frosting.

Well just goddamn.

"May I get you something, sir?" A blonde chick in an apron
was standing there, a pair of metal tongs in her hand.

"What are those?" I asked, pointing to the Black faces.

"Zwarte Pete."

"Zwarte-what?"

"They are named for Black Peter, who helps St. Niklaus
bring gifts to children."

"St. Nick had a slave?"

"Black Peter, along with the Black King Kaspar, are beloved
by the people of the Netherlands."

"And the Dutch people show their love for them with stuff like this?"

"Of course. Would you like to taste one?"

"Do I look like a fucking cannibal?"

I turned away and paced into an alley that reeked of marijuana. Some young cats were smoking joints at a table inside a coffeehouse, a neon cannabis leaf buzzing above the door. From inside I could hear Bob Marley singing "*It's all I ever have, redemption songs. . . .*"

I wished that I could step inside, sit down, and light up a spliff. I wished that I could go into a restaurant and knock down a double scotch on the rocks. I wished that I had bought a whole carton of Newports from the duty-free store at JFK. I wished—

"Oh—hello, Abel!"

I had almost walked into Sophie, who was coming down the street with a shopping bag in her arms. I hardly recognized her in her black leather jacket, her hair hidden beneath a French beret pulled down low over her eyes.

"What the hell are you doing here?"

"I'm on my way to visit someone."

"Well, ah—do you have some time, or could we, maybe, go somewhere and have a coffee?"

"Perhaps we could meet later."

"Where?" I tried not to sound too eager.

She thought for a moment. "Go right on the street in front of your hotel and cross the footbridge. You will come to Amsterdam's new opera house. There is a quiet café inside and I could be there in maybe one hour."

"I'll find it."

I found it, all right. Though I felt like I was losing it.

I was, after all, Abel Paulus Crofton. A man of silence. I never shared with anyone—not even Serge—what I *really* felt. I dated one woman—I think her name was Marlene—for more than six months before I told her jack about my childhood. It was twelve months before I mentioned to LaToya Jones that my mother was a white European who I couldn't even remember. And none of my women knew much of anything about my Thirst.

It was just too dangerous.

But in a quiet corner of the quiet café of Amsterdam's new Muziektheater, in the smoke of my Newports—and with Dave Brubeck playing in the background—I spilled the story of my life all over Sophie.

". . . . I don't know that much. But it seems that my father was in the service—in Germany, in Cologne—and he made a trip to Amsterdam with some of his buddies. I guess he liked it and decided to come back after he was discharged."

She was listening silently, ignoring the cranberry juice she'd ordered. She was dressed in a black turtleneck and trousers, and her wild hair was still hidden beneath her beret. In the light from the single candle on the table her face seemed younger, more open. But her eyes remained cool. She lit an unfiltered cigarette and brought it to her lips, the paper crackling as she drew in the smoke.

"He lived here with my mother. In Amsterdam. For about three years. Then he just up and left her. At least, that's what I figure. Took me with him. We settled in Harlem and first my grandmother and then my aunt raised me."

Sophie listened, her gaze never leaving my face.

"Louis—that was my father's name—well, he wouldn't ever talk about her. I mean, he would talk *around* her—telling me all the things he couldn't stand about women. But my mother? He wouldn't even tell me her name."

Sophie's eyebrows went up a fraction, but she remained silent.

"That's a hell of a thing," I murmured. "A father refusing to tell a kid his own mother's name."

Sophie again brought her cigarette to her lips.

"Not knowing about my mother wasn't so bad when I was a kid. Lots of kids in my neighborhood were missing a parent. And most of their fathers didn't even have jobs. At least Louis had regular gigs as a sax player. He would've been pretty good if he'd stayed away from the bottle."

I lit another Newport.

"Most of the time he was either gone or asleep or passed out. Except when he was pissed off about something. Then things could get crazy. So I got through my childhood by keeping my mouth shut and doing my best to blend into the scenery."

Sophie exhaled a ribbon of smoke.

"Now Grandma was different," I said. "Strictly old school. Deep South. Collard greens and chitlins. Lots of church. Spare the rod and spoil the child."

I smiled at my memory of the old woman in our kitchen, singing along with the radio as she peeled potatoes.

"She was a tough lady. She'd spank me with her mixing spoon if I got into something on the block. Then she'd bake me a cake from scratch and give me the same spoon so I could eat the leftover batter. And Louis was actually scared of her. He never hit me when she was around."

Sophie cocked her head, then glanced at the glass of juice at her elbow. It looked like wine in the candlelight.

"After my grandmother died there wasn't much left for

anybody to sing about. My father's sister came to live with us and she wasn't about to come up against my father. She spent her entire life at the cash register in a pharmacy, waiting for a man to find her and take her away. Problem was, that man hadn't even been born."

My words ended with a long silence. I stubbed out my cigarette and closed my eyes. Sophie touched my hand and I blinked quickly, glancing around at the café with its glass-topped tables and soft music. She was watching me real close.

"What kind of smokes are those?" I pointed to her crumpled blue pack.

"Gauloise. From France. Do you want one?"

I tapped the unfiltered cigarette on the table, then lit it.

"Damn, woman! This tastes like wet cardboard."

She smiled. "Why bother to smoke if you can't taste the tobacco?"

"That's alright—I'll stick to menthol."

I handed her the cigarette and lit one of my Newports. A tourist boat with swaying Christmas lights was gliding by on the canal outside.

"I sure am a long way from Harlem."

"Homesick?"

"I don't know. When I was a kid I'd go and sit on the wall overlooking the East River. I always dreamed about following that current just to see where I'd end up. When I got older I'd ride all the way out to Coney Island in the winter and walk alone on the beach. I guess I never was much good with people."

Our eyes met and I laughed in embarrassment. "I usually don't talk about myself like this."

"Why not?"

"Because nobody at home would want to hear it."

"Nobody?"

I gave a quick, hard grunt. "Well, Serge would let me talk all night if I wanted to. He's my spon— Well, he's my best friend."

"No wife?"

"No."

"Kids?"

"Hell, no!"

"Plans?"

"I've always wanted to write a book."

"About your life?"

"I don't know. I mean, who the hell would want to hear my story?"

"You don't have to write it for anyone else. You should do what you know is right for you."

"Well, that's for some time in the far and unforeseeable future."

She tipped her head and a veil of smoke passed before her eyes.

"The truth is that I like my life," I said. "I like being on my own. And I like my Harlem. Great clubs and good food. A place where a Black man can feel at home."

"So you've always lived there?"

"Never want to leave. I have a little place near a park. Cheap, comfortable and just big enough for me."

"Sounds good."

"That's right. There's nobody around to give me any shit. I mean, people with families get all caught up in wondering if their folks ever really loved them, or why nobody loved them enough, or what was wrong with them because their folks preferred some distant second cousin—" I laughed, shaking my head. "And the truth is that in this life you're on your own. I mean, nobody ever really gives a fuck about anybody but themselves."

Sophie put down her cigarette and looked out the window.

"How do you feel here in Amsterdam?" she asked.

"I always feel like I'm on the verge of recognizing something. But I don't remember shit."

"Perhaps you share your father's memories."

"The only things Louis Crofton remembered about Amsterdam was the liquor and the whores. My pop loved liquor and whores."

Sophie's juice was shimmering like a rosé. I started talking again.

"It's stupid, but I don't really know what I feel."

"Does being here make you sad?"

"Not really. But it does get confusing. It seems like everything brings back something that I haven't thought about in years."

"From your childhood?"

"Yes. And from my . . ." I still wasn't ready to talk about my Thirst. "Well, let's just say I've never been in a place where you can sit in an opera house in the middle of the night and watch boats floating by. And everything's so damn clean. So safe and polite and well organized. I mean, if you want to get high, you just go in a little shop and purchase your dope over the counter. No street hustlers trying to hold you up while you're buying your shit. And you can get all the sex you want just by window shopping. No poor ladies freezing on the street corners. And nobody here has curtains. It's like the Dutch have never even heard about getting robbed. Hell, most of your stores aren't even seriously locked up at night!"

She laughed softly. "It is true that the buildings look clean. The Dutch do feel safe in their homes. And no, you don't see many beggars. But my country has other faces, too. Believe me, Abel. There's plenty of crime and filth and fear."

"Woman, I'll bet you've never even seen the kind of shit that goes on in the States."

Sophie pushed a stray hair away from her eyes. "What kind of work do you do?"

"I've been laying cable for the electric company for twenty-five years."

"Twenty-five years?"

"A quarter century in the hole. I always thought I would quit, but it just never happened. Eventually my friend Serge convinced me to go back to school and I realized I liked it. I got my high school diploma and then went on with more electronics classes. Actually got an associate's degree. I'm one of the supervisors now, so I don't have to do the real shit work anymore. And the truth is that I never could see myself sitting in a white man's office. The money's not all that great, but I guess that in some way, the tunnels feel like home."

I looked at my scarred hands. "So that's how I've spent most of my life. When my father died last month I found out that although he never bothered to take out any life insurance, he had actually bought funeral insurance. So even though the bastard didn't leave me a dime, I managed to bury him in such a way that I could at least get myself on a plane and come looking for my mother.

"You know, I really think I'm here because—" I stopped in mid-sentence, surprised by the confession I was about to make. "Well, it's about a kind of loneliness."

"For your Dutch blood?"

"Not exactly. It's more like loneliness for someone who looks like me." I laughed. It was too stupid: a Black man looking for himself in a nation full of white people.

"It's true you look quite Dutch," she said thoughtfully. "I saw that right away."

"And it doesn't matter that I'm Black?"

"There are Dutch territories in the Caribbean. Aruba, Curaçao and Saba—"

"But white people don't really think of Caribbean people as *Dutch,* do they?"

"We know that the cultures are different, but they have the full rights of citizens when they live in Dutch territories."

"Well, Black people have been in America since before the *Mayflower* and we still don't have equal rights."

"We are a small nation, surrounded by big neighbors. Perhaps we feel the need to welcome all our people."

There was a coolness in her voice, so I decided to let it go. Anyway, I hadn't traveled to Amsterdam just to find some reason to diss it.

"Well, I'll say one thing," I murmured, looking into Sophie's eyes. "I've never met another woman as calm as you."

"It took me a long time to learn it."

"And how did you do that?"

"By fighting for the things I need to change, and accepting the things I can't."

"That," I said, looking at her with surprise, "can be difficult."

"It depends on whether one has the wisdom to recognize the difference."

"Sweet Jesus! You know the Prayer?"

"Know it?" Her smile deepened. "I live it."

"Shit—how long?"

"Seven years, four months and twenty-two days. And you?"

"Twelve years. But how did you know I—"

"Sometimes you just know."

"You serve alcohol in your café."

"Many people work in bakeries and never eat a sweet roll."

"But sugar's not the same as alcohol."

"It's not a question of temptation, Abel. It's a question of self-control."

"You could work somewhere else."

"Elias likes me to be there."

"Elias?"

"The man you met this morning. My husband."

Shit. I drew in my breath. I looked at her ringless fingers. Sophie raised the burned-out cigarette to her lips once more before pushing it into the ashtray. The smoke bloomed up and for a moment I couldn't see her eyes.

"I hope your husband wasn't too pissed off when I appeared at your door."

For the first time she seemed hesitant to reply. She glanced down, taking in her own long fingers. "Husbands can be difficult."

"I wouldn't know. I don't mess around with married women."

"I'm sure you don't have to. You are a very beautiful man."

"My face has nothing to do with it."

"And your beauty really has very little to do with your face."

"What?"

"I think that your face has been the source of a great deal of suffering in your life."

"What do you mean?"

"Most people are moved by what they see. It's easier than dealing with the man beneath."

"What makes you think that I'm different from what you see?"

"We all wear masks."

"Not everyone deserves to see who I really am."

"But it's in your eyes, Abel."

"What do you mean?"

"In your eyes I see loneliness and a quiet despair. I think

you have searched a long time for something—or someone—to trust."

I shifted in my chair, not sure what to say. Sophie bent down to light another cigarette. She exhaled slowly, then raised her head to look into my face.

"Abel," she said very softly. "Would you please make love with me?"

Sex is different when you're sober.

I mean, being drunk made it easy for me to do whatever I felt like doing, without giving a shit about who I was with. Take that thing with Petey Smith. Petey and I went way back, almost to my first days in the tunnel.

Petey got married to this beautiful girl, Crystal. She was a big girl, the kind of girl with big thighs and a big ass and an appetite for sex to match. Petey was real proud of her, and often brought her down to the bar to show her off right before we went on shift.

Problem was that Crystal didn't like Petey leaving her alone at night, so she expressed her anger by sleeping with nearly every man on our crew during the day. Sometimes a guy would get on the elevator at the start of the shift, say hello to Petey, then turn and wink at somebody else. We all knew what it meant: he had just been banging Crystal.

And hell, I'll admit that I was doing her, too. We'd hook up in the afternoon, in a hotel down on 118th. Polish off a bottle of Chivas while we were kicking it. I didn't know or care what Crystal was telling Petey. He didn't seem to suspect a thing when we'd all meet up at the bar a few hours later.

But then I got sober.

Some guys who get off the bottle just replace the bottle with sex. I've known guys who quit drinking, then went around fucking anything and everything they could find—like women were shots of liquor or something.

With me it was different. I just didn't want the hassles that came with juggling multiple partners at the same time. At the end of the day, fighting with a woman just made me want to drink, and I was having enough trouble getting on top of my Thirst as it was. So I kept things very simple and very clear: one woman at a time. No promises I couldn't keep. No illusions and no regrets.

But now I was faced with Sophie—a whole new ball game. Yeah, I wanted to fuck her. I'd been thinking about it from the moment I first laid eyes on her.

But sixty seconds before her request to have sex she'd been talking about her husband. And she was trying to pretend that it wasn't crazy for a recovering addict to be working in a bar. What kind of goddamn game was she playing?

Still, I paid for our drinks and we walked out of the Muziektheater and into the night. Some bossa nova started playing in my head again. We crossed the arched footbridge without speaking and returned to my hotel. I used my magnetic key to open the front door and we crossed the empty lobby in silence. We took the elevator to the fifth floor and entered my room. She removed her black leather jacket and beret and went into the bathroom. When she came out she walked to the bed and sat down.

I moved away from the window, which I'd opened just enough to let in the muffled bass pounding up from a disco below. Despite the lust that lurched up in my gut, I refused to give in so quickly.

"Where's your husband tonight, Sophie?"

"At Vetiver."

"Drinking?"

"Working. He owns it."

"I see. And where does Elias think *you* are?"

"He's my husband, not my master."

"That's why you're not wearing a wedding ring?"

"I'm not a complicated woman, Abel. If this isn't right for you, I'll leave."

Damn! Once again I didn't know what to say. I wanted her to stay—I wanted to press her hard on the bed and thrust all of my fears and frustrations into her. For I knew, even as we had left the opera house and crossed the bridge over that black water, walking so close together and yet so careful not to touch—yeah, I knew damned well that if Sophie hadn't turned up my Thirst might have taken me that night.

"I didn't say that you should go," I mumbled.

"It's okay. I can see you're not comfortable with this."

"I'm not comfortable with you being married."

"I understand."

"Wait," I began, but she was already standing up. Without another word she picked up her jacket. I stepped forward and touched her shoulder.

"Listen, Sophie. What goes on between you and your husband isn't my business."

"Of course not."

"I . . . I was attracted to you from the first moment I saw you . . ."—our eyes met—"but as a rule I don't mess with another man's wife."

"All right," she answered with a calm smile. She turned to go and helplessly I followed her to the door.

"You—you really don't have to leave."

"It's okay," she replied as she reached for the door handle. She turned her head to look at me. "I only came here because I know that loneliness you talked about. You don't have to worry—I'll be fine. It just seems that you're a better man than I'm used to."

She hoisted her bag to her shoulder. "*Goedenavond*, Abel."

"Wait," I whispered. There was a long silence. "Don't go."

Somewhere down the hall a door opened and slammed.

"Are you sure?" She didn't look up.

"Yeah, baby. I'm sure."

I woke up with a start and found myself alone. Traces of Sophie's melody were drifting about the room like smoke. I could still feel her touch on my body.

Turned out that she was Hancock's "Maiden Voyage." Soft. Bittersweet. Tender, yet somehow always distant.

She let me undress her. She took a couple of condoms out of her purse. I put on a glove and she smiled and offered that beautiful ass to me. Facing the mirror, she drew in her breath when I took her from behind, watching our faces in the low light. I held her breasts, and nearly lifted her off the floor, loving the way her hair felt against my skin.

She smiled, her dark eyes closing as her breath came faster. And I made it happen fast. At least, the first time.

Soon I was on my back and she was taking charge. The woman really knew how to make love—in fact, she read my body like we'd been kicking it for years. I couldn't believe what she made me feel: kind of a deep, smothering safety. Like this was the one sure thing in my life.

So I surrendered to my need, pushing up into her. I began calling her name and she made a soft sound and rode me harder. We exploded in silence, and when we moved apart, for a moment I felt like crying.

I must have fallen asleep. Suddenly I jerked awake and found myself alone. Drunken laughter and the sudden explosions of motorbike engines echoed up from the street. I lit a Newport and laid there, keeping my eyes away from the minibar.

I've experienced about every kind of loneliness known to man. But loneliness after sex is a motherfucker. Sometimes you fuck somebody and just want them to get the hell out of your bed. Other times you start making love with a woman and wish it would last forever.

Of course that's some stupid shit.

I know that the only thing that'll last forever is my Thirst.

So what am I supposed to do? Call the cops on myself? Sit down and try to remember every shitty thing I did to somebody since I was in diapers?"

"Something like that."

We were chilling in Serge's crib in Brooklyn, watching the Knicks getting their asses whupped by the Lakers. Angie was walking in and out, setting down bowls of peanuts and chips on the coffee table. We could hear her girlfriends in the kitchen giggling about something.

"Fuck all of that. I did what I had to do to stay alive."

"Of course, buddy."

"And nobody has a right to say a goddamn thing about it if they weren't there."

"You're right."

"So why would I even bother to go there?"

"Because you need to deal with it."

"Why? That shit is over. It's in the past."

Serge gave me his cut-the-bullshit look and took a swig of his Coke. I lit a cigarette and walked over to the window so I could blow the smoke outside—and to avoid his eyes.

It was hard for me to admit that I was stuck. That I had hit a wall, so to speak. Eighteen months of sobriety and I had finally made a truce with my Thirst: so long as I went to the meetings and got help from Serge when things got rough, I was managing to stay dry.

But there was always this other baggage. Old shit. Miserable stuff that I just wanted to forget. I mean, who gave a damn about the things I did when I was too drunk to see straight? Every drunk had blackouts. Every drunk made mistakes that were just like mine. But that crap was over. I was clean now.

I sat back down and tried to sound like I was fine with what I was saying.

"Look, Serge: I'm not making any lists of the shit I did when I was drinking."

"That shit can make it hard to stay clean."

"Why does everything about sobriety have to be so damn hard?"

"Because life is hard, Abe. We drank to avoid dealing with how hard it is."

"So now I got to deal with life, my Thirst and my past, too? Naw, man—that's like taking a cobra to bed with you."

He leaned toward me. "You may not want to hear this," he said, "but keeping the box locked won't protect you from shit. Some wounds won't stop bleeding until you start dealing with them."

"I've already got enough to deal with."

"There's no rush. You take it one day at a time, and when you feel ready, let me know and we'll start working on some of that stuff."

"There's no *stuff* to work on, Serge. I've made my peace with everything that happened and I'm not traveling down that fucked-up road again."

The Knicks managed to score and I pretended to cheer right along with the folks on the television.

It was just past nine in the morning. And I already wanted to kick somebody's ass.

To be more precise, I wanted to fuck up the piece-of-shit agent from the Ajax management office in Haarlem.

"I'm calling to inquire about someone named Justina Van Gelder."

"Who?"

"Justina Van Gelder."

"There is no one here by that name."

"I was hoping you could help me find her."

"But this is a property management office."

"Are you responsible for a house owned by Mrs. Van Gelder?"

"You said Justina Van Gelder?"

"Yes."

"No. We do not manage a house for Justina Van Gelder. Could you perhaps mean Maria J. Van Gelder?"

"Does that *J* stand for Justina?"

"That is not in my record."

"Does she have a house on the Laurier Weg?"

"Yes, but the house of Madame Van Gelder is not free."

"I'm not interested in the house. I'm trying to contact Mrs. Van Gelder."

"But Mrs. Van Gelder is not here. She is only a client of our agency."

"All right—"

"And there is no other house from Mrs. Van Gelder."

"I don't want to talk to her about a house."

"Then how can we help you?"

"I need an address or a phone number for Mrs. Van Gelder."

"But we have been engaged to take care of the house."

"I'm a member of her family and I'm trying to reach her."

"You are her relation but you don't know where she is?"

"Right. That's why I'm calling you."

"It would be better for you to go to the Registry—"

"I already did. They gave me the address of the house on the Laurier Weg."

"But Mrs. Van Gelder does not live there."

"I realize that {*goddamn it!*}. Listen {*you asshole*}, my father and I left Amsterdam in 1962. We haven't heard from her since that time and I really need to find her."

The fool didn't answer.

"Mister," I said, "I've been to the Registry in Amsterdam and the Registry in Haarlem, too. I've been through the phone books and I even talked to a woman who lives in the lower floor of her house. I'm only going to be here over the Christmas holidays and I just want to—to say hello to her. Can you *please* tell me how to reach her?"

No response. After a minute or so I thought I heard a file cabinet open, followed by the shuffling of papers. Then he came back on the line.

"Sir, are you there? This is a highly unusual request, but as you say you are a relation, I will try to help. Our records indicate that Maria Van Gelder's home was placed with us two years ago. She left an address in Zandvoort. I will give it to you now."

I dressed slowly and walked to Café Vetiver. It was still early and the place smelled of fresh coffee and cleaning solution. Someone had put sprigs of a purple flower into a little vase on each of the tables, and Paco de Lucia was playing in the background.

I slid onto a barstool and waited for Sophie to come out. There was no television behind the bar, so my eyes fell on the bottles of booze on the glass shelves. I didn't recognize many of them. It had never occurred to me that everybody in the world didn't get drunk on the same shit. I wondered if being drunk felt different in Amsterdam than it did in New York. Was it faster? Deeper? Sweeter? More sad? Shaking the thought out of my head, I looked up as someone walked out from the rear.

Instead of Sophie, Elias appeared with a tray loaded with baskets of sweet rolls and a tray of espresso cups. He placed the tray on the counter and turned to the sink to wash his hands. Then picking up a towel, he looked at me coldly.

"You wish to order?"

"Coffee. And one of those rolls." I kept my voice as neutral as if I was in a midtown diner dealing with a waitress who'd been on her feet all night.

Elias made the espresso and shoved a basket in my direction. Outside several students with backpacks rode by on bicycles, making a lot of noise.

"What do I owe you?"

"I don't know."

"Pardon me?"

"What are you paying for?"

"I'm paying for what I ordered."

"And nothing else?"

"Such as?"

"Maybe you are paying for Sophie."

Shit. Those two really don't fuck around.

"I don't know what you're talking about."

"Was she with you last night?"

"With me?"

"Did she sleep at your hotel?"

"No."

"She came in very early this morning and I thought—"

"Why don't you just ask her?"

"She will tell me only what she wants me to know."

That's your fucking problem. "Can't help you," I said with a shrug.

I took a sip of the bitter coffee and watched the Dutchman. He was watching me back.

"You and Sophie have become friends."

"Somewhat."

"Perhaps you met her at a meeting."

"No, I met her right here."

Elias looked out the window, his eyes hard. "My wife is very complicated. It is sometimes difficult to know what she is feeling. I think she has been more open with you than she is with many people—"

"We've only talked two or three times."

"But those talks have made a difference in her."

"How?"

His eyes snapped back to me. "You are a handsome man. Here in the Netherlands we find great beauty in mixed blood."

"So what?"

"You are also a survivor."

"What do you mean?"

"I mean that you were born, despite the fact that society in general is uncomfortable with mixed-race unions."

"That shit doesn't matter to me."

Elias smiled coolly. "But it does to Sophie. You see, my friend, my wife is always searching for a reason to stay clean for another day. A reason to come home even though she's been with another man."

"I don't know what you're talking about."

"You are looking for someone, here?"

"Yeah, but—"

"My wife is looking, too. The only difference between you is that she is looking for herself."

I got to my feet. "I don't know anything about your wife and I don't want to get involved with—"

Elias suddenly laughed. "Don't worry. No one can make Sophie do anything she doesn't want to do. I accepted that a long time ago."

I dropped some money on the counter and took a step toward the door. At the threshold I turned. "I need to get to a place called Zandvoort."

"Central Station. Train every half hour."

"Thank you."

"Please come again," the Dutchman replied.

I had taken only two or three steps when someone touched my arm. I found myself face-to-face with a Black woman—a homeless Black woman.

She was a bag of boney, ashy naps with rock-hard eyes and a junkie's jittery stare.

"Got some change, my brother?"

Beneath all the grime was a British accent.

I glanced up the sidewalk behind her, then took a quick look over my shoulder. The narrow passage was empty.

If she had been white I would have kept walking. But what in the hell was a Black woman from England doing in this alley begging for change?

I fished in my pocket. She waited, her stony eyes never leaving my face.

I put a couple of bills into her hand. She turned away slowly, took two or three twitching steps, and lowered herself to a doorway.

God bless the child who's got his own.

Sophie was right. This place wasn't what the tourist books cracked it up to be. Pun intended.

Zandvoort was a dinky little town facing the North Sea. The train station was located at the top of a street leading down to the wide, windy beach. It reminded me of Coney Island in the winter: a deserted walkway, shuttered-up french fry stands and some high-rise apartments standing alone on the horizon.

I kicked a rock aside as I moved slowly toward the sandy boardwalk. A canvas tarp snapped against its stays, billowing up to reveal chipped horses on an old merry-go-round. A few steps farther I paused to look at my reflection in a cracked carnival mirror.

In the warped glass my eyes looked like a puppy's sad stare. My jaw drooped down to my knobby knees. I lifted my hands, opened them slowly, and brought them to my cheeks. I tried out a smile, becoming a clown in blackface. Then I frowned. My eyes sank and my cheeks vanished into a death mask.

Something like Louis's face in his coffin.

The address the Ajax agency had given me matched a big modern brick building located just a block from the waterfront. Though I couldn't figure out the sign—ZIEKENHUIS ZANDVOOR— the place looked like a hospital.

I tried to look all Manhattan as I walked up the drive. I was scared shitless, but they didn't get to see it.

The doors opened up to a large day room. Several white-haired people were sitting together with open prayer books on their laps. Two women were knitting. An attendant was serving tea from a small cart in the rear. Hidden speakers were playing quiet classical music. The air smelled like roses.

I tried to catch the eye of one of the nurses, but no one seemed to notice me. Didn't anyone give a shit that a stranger had just walked in through the front door? A Black stranger, at that?

I finally cleared my throat real loud. Two or three of the white-haired residents looked up. They smiled. One man raised his hand in greeting. Another stared blankly.

And then it hit me: *Alzheimer's*. If my mother was here, she might not even know who *she* was—much less *me*.

I crossed the quiet room, the empty eyes following me. I approached the young woman serving tea and greeted her in English. She responded in Dutch and pointed toward a glassed-in office behind us.

A tall, forty-something woman in a dark suit got up from behind a desk and met me at the door. Her short gray hair and wire-framed glasses said authority, but she smiled and waved for me to enter.

"Excuse me. Do you speak English?"

"Yes. My name is Marta Blankenvoort. I'm the director of this facility."

"Abel Crofton." We shook hands and the woman sat down, motioning for me to take the chair just across from her.

"I'm a tourist from New York and I'm looking for an old family friend. Her name is Maria Justina Van Gelder."

"I see."

"Does Mrs. Van Gelder live here?"

She thought things over for a minute, then nodded. "Yes. Mrs. Van Gelder has been a resident here for several years. Would you like to speak with her?"

"Please." My voice had gone hoarse.

"I will see if Mrs. Van Gelder is well enough to have a visitor." She picked up her phone and talked for a while in Dutch. I felt my right eye twitching and hoped she didn't notice. When she hung up I leaned forward anxiously.

"Is this some kind of—hospital?"

"We are actually a residence for the elderly. Some of our guests are here for rehabilitation, but others simply choose to live here."

"Is Mrs. Van Gelder ill?"

The director paused for the first time. I figured she was trying to decide how much of my mother's private life she should disclose.

"You are a member of her family?"

"Mrs. Van Gelder and my father were very close many years ago. My father died recently, but he always spoke warmly of her. I thought I'd just stop in and spend a few moments with her while I'm visiting Amsterdam."

"I see. Well, Mrs. Van Gelder is recovering from a—let me see if I remember the correct word in English—a stroke? Yes, I believe that's right."

"A stroke."

"There was some paralysis, but she has her full mental capacity and understands things quite well. She does, however, have some difficulty with speaking."

I looked at the floor, trying to avoid the woman's eyes.

"Is this your first visit to the Netherlands, Mr. Crofton?" she asked quietly.

"No—well, yes. I mean, I was born here, but I haven't been back for over forty years."

"Then Mrs. Van Gelder is not expecting you."

"No."

We both stood as a nurse came to the doorway. She said something in Dutch and the director nodded.

"This nurse will bring you to our conservatory, where you can visit with Mrs. Van Gelder. I hope you enjoy your stay."

The nurse led me through the long corridors of the building.

I didn't hear any televisions, radios or loud voices. There was no smell of disinfectant. No orderlies laughing in the corners, like they laughed just outside the room where my father was dying. There were no vending machines selling sodas and junk food. This place seemed sealed off from the outside world.

We walked through a set of double doors and down a short hall that opened to a large glass dome filled with flowers. I recognized some of them, but there was plenty of shit in there that I had never seen before. I knew that Holland was famous for its tulips—there were tulips in many of the pictures I collected when I was a kid. But I had never seen anything like this.

The air was humid and almost sickly sweet. Ferns and palms reached up to the ceiling and pressed against the glass, changing the gray light to a soft green. Something yellow flew over my head and I saw a parakeet landing on the stem of a red flower. From somewhere beneath the thick leaves I could hear trickling water.

"Wait here, please," the nurse said, pointing me to a cement bench surrounded by pink bushes. Sinking down slowly, I breathed in the heavy air as she walked away.

My jacket felt like lead, so I took it off and laid it over my knees. After a few seconds I took my sweater off, too. The sweat was dripping into my shirt collar, and my fingers were tingling as I wiped it away.

Shit, I thought. I must look like a real fool.

Suddenly I heard the sound of doors opening, followed by the glistening of metal wheels. I braced myself, my fingers clutching the edge of the bench as I pressed my feet flat to the floor. I tried to breathe normally, but I was clenching my teeth so hard that I felt a spasm in my jaw.

The top of the nurse's head appeared from behind a vine of white flowers. Then I saw a pair of shoes on a metal plate, followed by thin thighs and finally the torso, shoulders and head of a woman in a light blue smock, her hands folded in her lap. She turned her head away as the wheelchair came closer, trying to get a closer look at a fat yellow flower.

The nurse pushed the wheelchair directly up to me and stepped on the brake.

"Do you need anything else at this time?"

I looked up at her. The roar in my ears was so loud that I just shook my head.

She nodded and walked away.

There was no sound except for the trickling water and my booming heart.

For what seemed like forever, neither of us moved. And then the woman in the wheelchair leaned slightly forward. Slowly. Painfully. Her head swiveled around like it was made of stone.

And I looked into my face. A face with heavy-lidded eyes. High cheekbones. A fine nose and prominent lips. Even my smooth skin. The woman's snow-white hair was clipped short and brushed away from her brows. She stared at me through ice blue pupils. The right edge of her mouth was drawn up tight, like a broken venetian blind.

I took a deep breath, trying to calm the roar in my head. My hands were shaking so much that I grabbed my knees, only to find them trembling. I was scared as hell that if I tried to speak I might start to cry.

We sat there for a while. Then the woman's lips parted and I heard her strange, stumbling voice: "*Begrijp ik niet.*"

I squinted, trying to make sense of her words. She repeated the phrase, then added, "*Au—gust?*"

What did she want to know? The month? The time of the year?

"December," I rasped, saying the word very slowly in the hope that she would understand my English. "It's almost Christmas."

She brought her brows together in a puzzled expression. Then she carefully lifted her limp right hand with her left, reaching over to place it on my arm.

"Who?"

I looked into her eyes, desperately searching for some sign of memory. But she was seeing something else—probably something that happened a long time ago.

"Mrs. Van Gelder—" I paused, pissed at myself for not knowing whether I should call her Mother. "I believe that I'm your—your son. I'm Abel Paulus. *Ah-bell Pow-loose.*" I tried to pronounce my name the way Sophie had, with a Dutch accent.

The woman froze, her eyes widening and her face taking on, for a second, an almost normal shape. She started breathing fast and she bent forward at the waist, moving closer to me. "A-bel?" The word was thick and low.

"Yes—I'm your boy, Abel Paulus. Louis Crofton was my father."

"Lou-is?" she whispered, closing her eyes and pulling her lips together tightly. I reached forward and she clutched my fingers with her good left hand. I felt her entire frame start to shake.

"You?" I heard the word pushed through her weak lips, and I stared back at her.

"You: Abel Paulus?" Her eyes searched my face.

I nodded, rising from my chair to kneel down on the cement floor beside her. "Yes. I'm Abel. I came here from America. From New York."

"New York?" The words were thick.

"I came here to—to find you."

She stared at me for so long that I wasn't sure she understood. I shifted my weight on the floor where my knees were starting to ache.

Then, with amazing tenderness, she reached up with her shaking fingers and touched my face. "My baby," she whispered.

That's when I lost it.

I began to cry like I hadn't cried since I was a kid. And she cried with me, her arms tight around my shoulders.

By the time the nurse returned I had cried my eyes dry. My mother was sitting in silence, her head bowed. She was still clutching my hands.

The nurse smiled at me kindly. "Sleep," she said quietly, indicating my mother.

I rose awkwardly as the nurse began to wheel the chair away. "Do you think she's all right?"

"Yes, I think so."

"May I—I mean, I can come again? Maybe tomorrow?"

Still smiling, the nurse nodded. "Please come back. It will be good for Mrs. Van Gelder to have a visitor."

I was almost taken that night.

Shaking and nauseous, I sat on the edge of the bed with my hands on my knees, breathing as slow as I could. When I started feeling calmer I ordered a sandwich from the hotel kitchen, then left it on the tray while I paced back and forth between the window and the bath.

Finally I turned on the television and laid there in the darkness with the sound off, watching the shifting blue and gray lights on the ceiling.

And along came Louis, showing up like he always did, right when I couldn't deal with him.

"So. You still laying cables, boy?"

I was standing beside him in a dark, noisy bar, just a few months before his death. I'd stopped by to hear him play in one of the few clubs that was willing to hire a musician who was usually too drunk to stand up.

"I finished my certification, Pop. I'm a Master Electrician now."

"But you still in the hole—"

"Yeah, I still work for the power company."

Louis pushed back his hat, a sweat-stained felt fedora he always wore whenever he performed. His fingernails were cracked and broken. The Kool in his hand shook gently.

"You ain't tired a crawlin' round in the dark like some goddamn roach?"

"I'm the supervisor, Pop. I don't have to do the heavy stuff anymore."

"Supervisor, huh? So you're just like a white man now."

"I'm just taking care of business, which is more than you ever managed to do."

"You still don' make enough bread to do shit."

"I make enough for everything I need."

"And that would be?"

"A job. A crib. A woman."

He leaned back against the counter and picked up his double bourbon. "To tell you the truth, son, I can't believe any bitch would have nothing to do with you. You always been strange. You got that white woman face with brown skin. And god knows you ain't got no talent. Couldn't play a note on a horn or even find the beat on a drum if you tried."

He drained the glass and set it down on the counter. "And you can't even hold your liquor! I don't know how you ever called yourself my son!"

Well, Louis, I don't have to call myself your son anymore, I thought as I stared at the hotel ceiling.

After all this time I finally have a mother.

Still—it just wasn't enough.

My Thirst surged up like a claw in my gut, and my eyes instantly leapt to the minibar beneath the television. The memory of gin and tonic flooded my mouth with saliva.

Hands shaking, I reached for the phone beside the bed and pressed 0. The switchboard answered and I asked the voice to get me through to the U.S. After a series of clicks a phone began to ring. I waited, my breath so loud that I could barely hear the distant bleating. Then Serge's voice picked up: "Hey, friend! I'm either in the can or busy with my lady. Leave your number and I'll get right back to you—"

I slammed down the phone. Sweat broke out on my forehead and I laid very still, fighting my need to empty every bottle in that fucking cabinet.

Suddenly I heard a knocking so soft that I wasn't sure whether I'd imagined it. Breathing hard, I climbed off the bed and found Sophie standing in the corridor.

She came in quickly, smelling like the cold December night. As she pulled off her beret, her frizzy hair sprang to life around her face. I got hard just looking at her.

She let me kiss her, but when I slipped my hand beneath her sweater she pushed it away.

"I can't stay long. I have to open the café tomorrow morning."

"We can work that out." I brought my lips to her neck.

"No, Abel—" She took a step back. "I mean it."

"So tonight's your husband's turn, right?"

"You don't own me," she said softly, "and I'm not for rent by the hour."

I turned away, the minibar in my sight. She followed my gaze.

"What happened?"

"I found my mother. She lives in Zandvoort. She had a stroke and she's in a wheelchair. But I think she understood who I am."

"Oh, Abel—that's great." She reached up and touched my face. "What does she look like?"

"Like me, I guess. I mean, she has my nose and my eyes—except that her eyes are blue."

"And her hair?"

"It's white. Could be curly. I don't know—it's cut real short—"

"And was she glad to see you?"

"Yeah. I think so. Yeah."

I looked down at Sophie and remembered my mother's twisted mouth. I walked over to the open window and welcomed the cold.

"What's wrong?"

"Wrong? Well, nothing, except that she can hardly talk and I don't know how much English she understands."

I heard Sophie sink down on the bed. "You need to give her time."

"Time? After forty-three years I shouldn't be in a rush, right? I should just accept the fact that I might never find out what I really need to know."

"Isn't it enough that she's alive and recognizes you?"

"No. I want her to tell me why she let that bastard take me away."

"I see. You're trying to decide who you should blame for your childhood."

"I have a right to know. He refused to tell me anything, and I haven't come this far to go home with nothing."

"Nothing? Finding your mother is already a miracle."

"But if I give up without knowing the rest, then Louis wins. And that would be the shittiest joke that life could play on me."

"It would be much shittier if she was already dead."

"But that's just it. I could have come here years ago. If I'd had the guts to go looking for the truth, he wouldn't have had so much power over me. And maybe she would have been healthy enough to explain."

"Maybe you weren't ready to hear it."

I turned around in anger but lowered my eyes when I found Sophie staring at me.

"You have to accept the things you can't change, Abel."

"But this may be my only chance to know."

"Then don't waste it by being angry."

"I have a right to be angry."

"Your anger is destructive. It will only bring you more pain."

"You don't understand a goddamn thing about that."

"I know that most anger is rooted in guilt. If you can forgive yourself, then you'll be ready to forgive others."

"I have no intention of forgiving Louis Crofton."

"What is it, Abel? Are you afraid of the parts of your father you see in yourself?" She stood up and put on her jacket.

"Hang on, Sophie—"

"I have to go."

"Not yet."

"If I stay we'll end up making love."

"I won't try—"

"You won't have to. I want to be with you."

I went over to her and she let me slip my arms around her waist. "Come on, baby."

She took a step back and carefully removed my hands. "There are many reasons for two people to be together. Loneliness is one of them. Last night we needed each other, but tonight is different."

"I don't want to be alone right now."

"I know," she replied, zipping up her jacket. "But there are things you need to work out for yourself."

"I need you, Sophie."

She laughed softly. "Men always need a woman when they're afraid of something."

I watched as she gathered up her wild hair and pulled on her beret. She opened the door, then paused. "Meet me at Vetiver's at one o'clock tomorrow afternoon. I'll come with you to Zandvoort. Perhaps if I translate we can learn something more from your mother."

"Sophie, I—" Raising her hand, she went on speaking.

"I can give you the afternoon. But I have to be back in Amsterdam by five o'clock for my meeting. Do you understand?"

I nodded.

"And remember," she added. "You can handle this."

There's shit you tell and shit you don't.

Who wanted to hear that there was ice on the inside of the windows of our place when I came in from school, or that there was nothing to eat? Who gave a shit if Louis beat me with his belt for waking him up by flushing the toilet in the morning—but also beat me if I didn't flush it?

Nobody wanted to hear that my grandmother often got held up by the white family whose crib she cleaned, so she didn't get home until night. She wanted to quit but couldn't because they paid better than most and sent me all of their little boy's clothes when he got too big for them.

Later on Vanelle had shit to do with her girlfriends and didn't care too much about what was going on with me. By then I was living off the chicks I was screwing anyway. I wasn't real different from most of the guys on the streets, except that my looks got me over better than most.

And I didn't have a mother. But who gave a shit about that?

So when I shared at my meetings I told them all about my years on the bottle. But I never bothered to talk about my childhood.

There are things you tell. And things you don't.

———————

"Frau Van Gelder?"

Sophie's voice vibrated in the humid air of the conservatory. The old woman reluctantly gave up her view of my face to focus on the Dutch speaker.

Sophie began to talk very slowly, explaining who we were and why we had come. Maria Justina nodded stiffly.

"You think she understands?"

"Yes. What do you want me to tell her?"

"Tell her—tell her that I grew up in New York, and that when my father died I came here to find her."

Sophie delivered the message and we waited to see if Justina was able to reply. There was a long, painful moment of silence before the old woman pushed a few words out of her twisted lips.

"Never forget," Sophie translated. "She says that she's never forgotten you."

"Tell her my father wouldn't tell me anything about the past. I didn't know where she was or how to find her."

Again Sophie translated. A tremor passed across my mother's face. Again, with difficulty, she spoke.

"She thought you were dead," Sophie explained. "She never heard from your father and she had no idea where he'd taken you."

"I want to know what happened between them," I said. "Why did he leave? Why did he take me to America?"

Sophie put the question to my mother, who closed her eyes tightly. I shifted impatiently and Sophie silently touched my arm.

Slowly my mother held out her trembling hand. I took it, wrapping my fingers around hers. She said one phrase, then repeated it over and over again.

"She's saying something about the police," Sophie explained.

"The police?"

"Yes. Perhaps he had trouble with the immigration author-
ities."

"But they were married. Wouldn't he have had the right to
live here?"

"Yes. Maybe it had something to do with the military."

"No. I found his discharge papers when I went through his
things. If he left, it must have been for some other reason."

We both looked at my mother, who had lowered her eyes.

"Frau Van Gelder," Sophie said gently. The old woman
looked up. Sophie began to speak very slowly and quietly.

Again we waited through a long, difficult silence. Justina
said a few words, then stared at me intensely.

"She says she's very happy you're here."

"But did she say anything about my father?"

Sophie asked my mother a few more questions, and she struggled to reply.

"She wants you to come back tomorrow. She apologized for
being so tired."

I nodded reluctantly, still holding on to my mother's hand. She
worked her mouth, her eyes fixed on my face. "Au-gust. Au-gust—"

"Why does she keep saying that? Doesn't she realize it's December?"

Touching my arm, Sophie stood up to ring for a nurse. "Don't
be too disappointed, Abel. Your mother really isn't well."

Outside the sky was dark and the air smelled like rain. We
both pulled our collars up against the wind as we walked back
along the deserted boardwalk.

"I can't deal with this shit, Sophie. I'm so close, but I'm just
not getting through to her."

"You can't just show up after forty-three years and expect
everything to be simple."

"You don't fucking understand."

"If you can't accept things the way they are, then do something to change them."

"Such as?"

"Go back to the Registry in Amsterdam. See if they have any records on your father."

"You think they'll have something on Louis after all these years?"

"The Dutch are a very detail-oriented people. If your father lived here, they have his records."

We made the trip back to Amsterdam in silence. Even though my head was filled with thoughts about my mother, I kept staring at Sophie. She was sitting across from me, watching the passing fields. Her lips were slightly parted and her eyes had grown soft. Almost childlike.

"What's going on, baby?"

She glanced at me. Her face hardened.

"Nothing."

"Nothing what?"

"Nothing important."

"What were you thinking about?"

"I was just—I think you call it 'daydreaming.' "

"About what?"

"About something that can never happen."

"Come on, Sophie. You won't even share your daydreams with me?"

"It would be a waste of time."

"Why?"

"Because they're dreams now and they'll still be dreams when you're gone."

I reached over and took her hand. She pulled her fingers away.

"I only get to touch you after dark?"

"You only get to touch me when I'm ready."

"And what's wrong with now?"

"I guess it's you who doesn't understand."

"Meaning?"

"We had sex. Let's not pretend it was something else."

We parted on the steps of the Family Registry. Sophie had grown as cold and distant as she'd been the first time we'd walked through Amsterdam. She hardly looked at me as I thanked her for going with me to Zandvoort, and she turned away before I could say good-bye.

Well, fuck you, too, I thought as she walked off. I don't need to be bothered with your moody ass, anyway.

Soon I was filling out paperwork. I handed the forms to a clerk and took a seat in the waiting room. About fifteen minutes later someone called my name and I went up to the window. A middle-aged man in glasses—clearly some kind of supervisor— was standing there.

"Do you have some identification?"

I nodded, surprised. The first clerk hadn't asked me to prove my identity. I fumbled in my pocket and pulled out my passport. The man looked through it carefully, then typed my name, birth date and passport number into the computer.

"What are you doing?"

"The information you are asking to see is confidential. I must keep a record of who has access to it."

"What do you mean, confidential?"

"Only the police and the subject himself may read this file."

"The subject—that is, my father—is dead."

"You have a death certificate?"

"No. I mean, yes, but it's in America."

"What was the date of his death?"

"November second of this year."

The supervisor again turned to the computer, typing for several minutes while I waited. He finally spoke. "I am permitted to share this information with you, but only because our records do indicate that you are the son of the individual you are researching."

The man placed a thick manila folder on the counter. I saw my father's name and birth date printed on the top. He opened it to some pictures of my father in uniform.

"What's this?"

"It is a file on your father compiled by the police."

"The police? Why?"

The man ran his finger along several paragraphs written in Dutch. His eyes returned to my face.

"This document says that your father was the prime suspect in a crime committed in 1962. He then vanished and was assumed to be a fugitive."

"A fugitive? What was the crime?"

"Murder."

I thought I heard him wrong.

"Did you say he killed someone?"

"The report indicates that Louis Crofton was involved in an assault here in Amsterdam. He allegedly used a knife to attack another man."

"He stabbed someone?"

"The man died."

My heart hit the floor. With a dry mouth, I managed to raise my eyes.

"Who was the victim?"

"A father of three children. He lived in another flat in the same house as Mr. Crofton."

"Why did he do it?"

"The police do not know. The records show that Mr. Crofton was married to a Dutch woman—"

"Maria Justina Van Gelder?"

"Yes."

"Was she involved in the incident?"

"No. She was not in Amsterdam at the time."

"Was Louis Crofton arrested?"

"He was never found after the murder."

"What happened to his wife?"

"It appears that she obtained a divorce by reason of desertion and remained in the Netherlands with her child. That is the only information I have."

I felt as though a volcano had erupted and hot lava was spilling over my entire world.

Now I understand, you goddamn motherfucker! Of course you wouldn't talk about your past—you murdered someone and abandoned your wife! You couldn't even make contact with her, because for all you knew she might turn your fugitive ass over to the police! So you just hid out in New York and beat and starved your child and drank yourself to death—

I looked up to find the man still staring at me. "Well . . . well thank you for the information."

He closed the file and handed me a card. "Please send a copy of Mr. Crofton's death certificate to this office. It will allow us to officially close the case."

"Yeah, sure."

I had nearly reached the door when something suddenly snapped in my mind. I turned around and jogged back to the counter.

"Excuse me. You said that Maria Justina Van Gelder remained in the Netherlands with her child."

"Yes. That is what the records say."

"But that's not possible. I grew up in America."

The man again opened the file and read it carefully. "That is not the case. Louis Crofton left his wife and son behind."

"I'm telling you that I grew up in the United States."

"May I again look at your papers?"

The man studied my passport, then typed for several minutes.

"I am sure that what you are saying is true," he said, calmly meeting my eyes. "But a son of Louis Crofton and Maria Justina Van Gelder remained here in Holland."

"Your files must be wrong."

"That is unlikely, Mr. Crofton."

"Then what's the son's name?"

"His name is August Sebastian Van Gelder."

"August?"

"Yes. His birth date is July 11, 1960."

"That's not possible."

"Why not?"

"Because July 11, 1960, is *my* birthday."

August.

I dodged the rush-hour traffic, crossed a five-lane boulevard and ran into the main post office. After rifling through the Amsterdam phone directories I turned to Haarlem's and then to Zandvoort's to search for the August Sebastian Van Gelder who the clerk had identified as my brother.

My goddamn *twin.*

This is fucking crazy, I thought as I stood in the center of the post office, people pouring around me.

There's no such person as August Sebastian Van Gelder. All

of this has to be some kind of mistake. Because even if somebody was pathetic enough to have to live with that name—and I
thought *Abel Paulus* was bad—he would have to be my long-lost
cousin. Maybe an uncle, twice removed. Or maybe this is just a
strange misspelling of my own name. You know: Abel, August,
Abel, August. Some clerk got it mixed up forty-five years ago—

And no matter how hateful Louis Crofton was, he couldn't
have taken to his grave the fact that he'd fathered another son.
That I really wasn't alone—

I burst out of the post office and ran into the falling darkness.
I again survived a rush of cars in front of Amsterdam's Central
Station, and hurried to find a train that would take me back to
Haarlem before their Registry closed.

The clerk was already putting on her coat as I stormed into
the office. She looked up—it was clear she recognized me—and
tried to mask her irritation.

"I am sorry, sir. We are closed."

"I only need one thing—an address. Look: I have a name—"

The woman hesitated, then reluctantly approached the
counter. She read the paper I'd brought from Amsterdam.
Punching the information into her computer, she stared into the
screen with a frown.

"The file for this person is sealed."

"What does that mean?"

"It means that the government—probably the police—have
made it confidential for legal reasons."

"Such as?"

"This person was in some kind of difficulty. Perhaps he is in
prison."

"What was his crime?"

"The file does not say."

"Then there's no address?"

"No."

"Could he be dead?"

"Unlikely. But it is very late, sir. If you want to be sure, you will have to come again tomorrow."

Outside a thin rain was falling and the streets were nearly empty. I set out walking.

Just as I reached the terminal I recognized a voice.

"Hey, Abel! Hello! Remember me? It's Matthias. Matthias Ostern."

The kid who'd spoken to me two days earlier walked up, his hand raised in greeting. "You have come to Haarlem again!"

"Sure seems like it."

"You have found the person you seek?"

I thought I had until about an hour ago. "Yeah—as a matter of fact, I did."

"And now everything is okay!"

Actually, everything is fucked up. "Right."

The young man gestured toward four kids standing near the ticket windows. "We go to Amsterdam now, for dinner. Will you come? My friends speak quite good English." He laughed shyly. "At least, they speak better than me."

My first instinct was to refuse. But then I had nowhere else to go, and I sure as hell didn't feel like being alone.

Soon I was in a train compartment with a group of kids who were talking to me so fast that I could hardly keep up. Two of the young women seemed to be girlfriends of Matthias and his friend Markus, but there was another girl who looked on without speaking.

"And have you ever been to the Statue of Liberty?"

"Once, when I was a kid."

"Only once? But you live in New York."

"That's right."

"You should go all the time!"

"Why? Last time I looked it was the same statue."

"You see the shows on Broadway?"

"I hate musicals."

"But you watch the Knicks at Madison Square Garden?"

"I watch the Knicks on my television."

They looked at each other in surprise.

"You were there when the towers fell?" one of the girls asked softly.

I nodded.

"You were afraid?"

"Actually, I was asleep."

"Asleep?"

"I work at night, so I was out cold when all that shit went down."

"But you were in New York."

"I was in Harlem."

"That is also in New York, yes?"

"Yes, but Harlem is a different world."

There was silence, then Matthias asked what I meant.

"Well, a lot of Black folks are used to living in fear. I mean, a cop will blow your head off in New York for nothing. You can work hard your whole damn life and never be able to afford a place in Manhattan. To tell you the truth, the attacks didn't change much of anything for Black people."

"You weren't angry at the terrorists?"

"Yeah, I guess. But I wasn't real surprised."

"What do you mean?"

"Look, America's been doing shady shit to people all over the world for a long time. It just seemed logical that one day somebody would strike back."

"Then you agree with the terrorists?"

"No. But I can't say I don't understand them."

The kids couldn't go there. After a few moments Matthias politely changed the subject.

"You have seen the Grand Canyon?"

"In pictures."

"Yellowstone Park?"

"Cartoons. I think Yogi Bear hung out there."

"Mount Rushmore?"

"Hell, no."

"Why not?"

"That's just a bunch of white men. Now if Malcolm or Martin was up there it might be worth the trip."

"But you are all American," Matthias commented.

"There are many different Americas in my country."

"You mean, like north and south?"

"I mean like Black and white and Chinese and Indian."

"Still, you are all American."

"Maybe."

That kept them quiet for a few minutes.

"You have surely been to Hollywood," one of the girls finally remarked.

"I don't even go to the movies."

"Las Vegas?"

"Do I look rich?"

They laughed. "Come on! Americans make much money!"

"Not all Americans."

"You drive big Cadillacs!"

"I don't even have a car."

"You can't drive?"

"Don't need to. I take the subway."

"You perhaps know some famous persons in America?"

"I've never even seen a famous person. I'm just an ordinary guy from Harlem—"

"Oh, wow!" they exclaimed, laughing loudly.

"That's right. And believe me, your Haarlem is nothing like my Harlem."

"But you like our Haarlem, don't you?" Matthias asked. "Most tourists say it is a friendly city, unlike Amsterdam."

"That's right." I began to laugh, too. "Your Haarlem feels just like home."

The young people began talking to each other very rapidly in Dutch. Then, turning away from the window to fix her gray eyes on my face, the girl named Marieke spoke for the first time.

"Perhaps the Haarlem in the Netherlands is calling to the Harlem in you."

Maybe, I thought. Just maybe.

I went with the kids into a crowded pizzeria on the Rembrandt-splein, not far from my hotel. My new friends helped me order, then giggled when I asked for a soft drink instead of wine. I only half-listened to their fantasies of traveling in the United States, using their excited chatter to give myself time to think.

What had the Registry clerk said? *"This person was in some kind of difficulty. Perhaps he is in prison. . . ."*

"Abel?" It was Matthias, his face flushed from the dark beer he'd drunk down as soon as the waitress had brought it. "Don't you think Michael Jackson is the King of Pop?"

"Sure."

"No, no!" one of the girlfriends disagreed. "In the old days it was Elvis. Now it's Justin!"

Her words were met with a roar of disgust by the others. I

looked away in amused irritation and found Marieke staring into my eyes.

I knew that look.

She was taller than the others and nicely built; the candles on the table brought out the reddish tones in her dark wavy hair. She was wearing a skirt, and she was making sure that I could see quite a bit of thigh. Now she uncrossed her arms so I could enjoy that sweater, too.

All I would have to do was mention the name of my hotel and she'd show up as soon as she could ditch her friends. Then I could get a little action that night.

Someone called my name from the other end of the table and I blinked in surprise, realizing that I was staring back at Marieke.

"Abel!" Matthias shouted drunkenly. "Do you like the television program *Baywatch*? I think it has the most beautiful women in the world!"

I needed to go someplace and be around adults. Somewhere that wouldn't incite me to cradle robbing. I suddenly remembered that Club Coltrane was just a few steps away.

As I left the table, Matthias thanked me for coming to visit Haarlem. He was still thanking me while I shook hands with the other young people, carefully avoiding Marieke's eyes. Then I went out into the night.

There was this one girl. Kenya Montague. I remember that the night I met her, I could hardly wrap my mind around her name. She was fucking beautiful—an African princess with short, natural hair and the most perfect brown skin I had ever seen. She was tall, but she had some flesh on her. Wore her outfits like they were painted on her body. And she looked as good undressed as she did on the street.

Problem was, Kenya was Somebody's Daughter. Her father was a big-time lawyer who had served on the city council a few times. Name in the paper every day. Networked up to his balls with the mayor, heads of corporations and every private business owner in Harlem.

I spied Miss Kenya as she was walking down the avenue. I had a nice buzz on from a couple of whisky sodas and I was on my way to see Lionel Hampton downtown. We took one look at each other and I threw the ticket in the gutter and swore I would follow her to the ends of the earth—as long as they led to her bedroom.

We kicked it hard for about six months. And then she started talking about moving in together. Me getting out of the tunnels and going back to school. Letting her father set us up in a business. Wedding invitations, honeymoon resorts and what to name the babies.

And I knew I had to book. I mean, I didn't know who the hell that woman thought she was in love with. She didn't seem to notice that I had to get drunk to go to sleep and drunk to go to work and drunk to make love and drunk to walk straight. She didn't seem to care that the only things I cared about were music and liquor. And she clearly didn't realize how quiet I got when she started making plans. I mean, she was talking to herself. And I was right there in the room.

It was necessary to make her understand that she had chosen the wrong guy. So I invited her best friend up to my apartment one day and made sure I was fucking her when Kenya arrived.

I actually enjoyed what went down that afternoon.

And later, as I was finishing off a fifth of bourbon, I was glad I had liquor around to keep me from thinking about what was really happening inside of me.

The streetlights in front of Club Coltrane seemed blurred in the wet air. A fistful of people gathered there, passing around a bottle of beer. ERICH VAN ARNHEIM AND THE SAXMEISTER was written on the marquee, but there was no photograph of the musicians. In other words, no promise of anything but half-assed music. Local Dutch yokels wishing they were in a real bar. On a real stage. A New York stage.

Still, I paid the cover charge and went inside. No matter how bad the musicians were, this had to be better than my hotel room.

Inside, the club was nothing but shadows. Knee-high tables painted red and black made the room look like a giant checkerboard with a stage in the middle. A drum kit stood solitaire beside a tenor sax; a single spotlight hit the instruments.

Many of the tables were already taken. The folks were drinking beer or red wine. Seemed like everybody was smoking. The crowd was hard to place: too old to be students, too shabby to be white collar. The perfect place for me—except that nobody else was Black.

I took a seat at an empty table near the exit and a woman in a low-cut black dress sat down beside me.

"*Vous avez du feu?*"

"Uh, English—"

"*Ah, vous êtes Américain!*" She waved an unlit cigarette and I took out my crumpled pack of Newports and my lighter.

"I never see you here before," she remarked once our cigarettes were lit.

"Just visiting."

"*Alors*—you like jazz? They are very good musicians, here. They play in London and New York."

"New York?"

"Yes. The sax man is very great. He will one day be famous." Her words came out in little mushroom clouds.

A waiter showed up and I ordered a cola. The place was now nearly full. Couples slid into the small spaces between the tables, their arms and knees touching the people seated at the next table. Somebody would get shot if they put the tables this close at the clubs I went to at home.

"So you are a tourist?" the woman continued, placing a long-nailed hand on my arm.

"Right."

"Then you should visit Belgium. It is also very beautiful."

"I'm sure it is."

"Brussels is a very international city with many great artists and filmmakers. And you have good jazz music in my home, Anvers. I sing at a club there."

"Do you?"

"I am only in Amsterdam for a meeting about a recording contract. To be honest, this city is much too big for me. I always feel so lonely when I'm here."

The cola arrived with a wedge of lime floating in the glass. That pissed me off, but the waiter had already walked away.

"You are in Amsterdam alone?" The woman had moved closer. I could see the dark shadow between her breasts.

"Yeah." I took a sip of the cola. It actually tasted pretty good.

"So you need someone to show you around."

I could smell the scotch on her breath. She nudged me. "My hotel isn't too far from here. Maybe after some music you can come and have a drink——"

A white guy with bench-pressed biceps sat down behind the drums and picked up the sticks. Behind him a Black dude came into the light. Tall and bone-thin, he was wearing a ragged denim jacket with the collar pulled up to his jaw. His face was hidden by a low-slung fedora, the brim turned down to shade his cheeks. He placed himself on the edge of a stool and picked up the saxophone.

The crowd kept right on talking, as if the musicians were invisible. I wished I'd sat closer to the front, but it was too late—the club was full.

The drummer hit a trill on the snares, slashing out a bright introduction that brought the conversations to an abrupt halt. After a few more snaps, he launched into a waterfall of sound from the drums to a conga at his side. The sax player sat still, head lowered, the mouthpiece poised on the only part of his face I could see—his swollen lower lip. The drummer hit the conga with a sharp thump.

The sax whimpered out a kind of soft echo that slid into a

few whispery notes, then wound its way around the drum lines and into a melody. Still barely moving, the musician lifted his instrument into the white light and for a moment the room hung on the wave of sound. I closed my eyes, deciding to let go of my troubles for a little while.

"*So, Sophie—what if we tried living together?*"

The fantasy came out of nowhere.

"*Living together?*"

She's lying on top of me, her breasts pressed against my chest. I'm breathing in the scents of her warm skin and soft hair.

"*Sure, baby. Just you and me. In Harlem. My Harlem.*"

"*You know that can't happen.*"

I start stroking her ass and she sighs and rolls her hips against me.

"*Why not? New York's only a few hours away.*"

"*But Abel, I hardly know you—*"

I feel myself getting hard.

"*I can take care of that.*"

"*I'm married, baby.*"

She lifts her head and we kiss. Her nipples brush against mine.

"*I can make you happier than he does.*"

"*It's not that easy.*"

"*It could be,*" *I say and she sits up and straddles me.* "*Come on, baby. You just pack your things and we'll get on the plane.*"

She laughs and starts to work it nice and slow. "*And what would I do in your Harlem?*"

"*Just be my woman,*" *I say as I take her breasts in my hands.*

"*And what about your other women?*"

"*There's nobody else. I swear to you on my dear daddy's grave—*"

Suddenly my head snapped up and my thoughts came back into sharp focus. I recognized the song being spun from that wicked, tragic sax.

I knew that song in the marrow of my bones. I'd listened to it on countless childhood nights as my father blew it drunkenly into his own gin-soaked sax. It was the song I'd had them play at Louis's wake: John Coltrane's masterpiece, "A Love Supreme."

Suddenly I was on my feet. I began pushing myself through the crowded tables toward the stage. People shouted as I shoved knees and shoulders out of my way, all the while keeping my eyes on the gleaming horn beneath that low-brimmed fedora.

I stopped just short of the stage and waited, facing the sax player. The man swayed loosely forward, reaching for the high note that crested at the end of a phrase. I waited, eyes riveted on the thick, square-tipped fingers and blackened nails. Hands that made art out of pain.

And then the applause started and the hat came up and I saw my father stare down at me from beyond the grave. Louis Crofton's eyes were there, on the sunken face of the musician—but I still couldn't see much more.

I stood like a fool beside the stage, my head spinning as the applause died away. The sax player stared back at me. Then he lifted his horn, and still looking into my eyes, nodded to the drummer. The first notes of "Round Midnight" filled the smoky room.

Someone in the back called out in English for me to move. I glanced around, realizing that I was blocking the view of half the club. A guy sitting just beside me stood up and moved away, gesturing for me to take his seat.

When the set ended the crowd rose to stretch while the drummer waved a stubby arm over his head and walked out. Ignoring me, the sax player peered out over the spotlight and into the crowd, like he was looking for someone. Then he stepped off the stage, rolling his shoulders loosely.

In the darkness outside the club a few people surrounded him, offering him cigarettes and swigs of beer. I stood just outside the group, hoping to speak to him alone before he went back inside. A light rain began to fall and the other people moved toward the entrance. He started walking, too, glancing into the shadows.

"How you doing?" I asked.

His face still hidden, the sax player turned slowly toward me. He grunted softly.

"I enjoyed the music. I been digging Coltrane for a long time."

Silence.

"You ever played in the States? I thought I might have caught you in New York."

He looked up and I saw his shoulders tense.

"So what's your name? The poster over there says you call yourself the Saxmeister."

The man squinted at me, raising his hands slightly. "Don't got no cash, man." He had a British accent.

"I don't want money. I just want to know your name."

"For what?" The rain splashed off the brim of his hat, making it nearly impossible to see his face in the darkness. I took a step closer and kept my voice friendly.

"My name is Abel Crofton, and—"

There was a choking sound that might have been a laugh, and the musician took a damp pack of cigarettes from his pocket. Bringing the pack up to his mouth, he pulled a cigarette out with his teeth. His other hand emerging with a lighter.

"—and I thought your name might be August."

"What?" He flicked at the lighter with a black thumbnail.

"August Van Gelder."

The lighter flared and he sucked in the blue flame.

"No."

"Look, man," I said, speaking louder. "My father died a few

weeks ago and I came here from New York to look for my mother. I found her in a hospital in Zandvoort. And then I learned that I have a brother named August."

"So you see a Black man and think he must be your brother."

"No. I see a Black man who looks like my father and plays the same instrument and—"

"So fucking what?"

"So here I fucking am!"

We stared at each other, the rain pouring off our clothes. Then the musician raised his hands.

"No cash."

I wanted to snatch that hat off his head so I could get a good look at his face—but I controlled myself.

"Look, man—I don't want your money. I just want to talk."

The sax player looked directly at me. The rain got heavier and we stood like statues, eyes interlocked. The whole square was empty now except for the two of us.

Suddenly my instincts, honed from years of working on the nighttime streets, warned me that someone else was around. I looked over the musician's shoulder and saw that a small man in black clothes and a knit cap was standing close behind him. Too close. Seeing my surprised expression, the sax player looked back.

The two started arguing in Dutch. The musician kept shaking his head. Then the small man moved forward with the kind of compacted speed developed over a lifetime of fighting. Backing into me, the musician tried to duck. But it was too late.

The white cat hit the sax player in the center of his chest and both of us went down on the street. He hauled the musician up from the ground and started kicking him, all the time shouting something.

I scrambled up and tried to pull the men apart. But the little guy was quicker than me.

I heard a sharp click and stumbled back as the reflection of a blade sliced the light. The sax player rolled over dizzily and tried to stand. The white cat's arm swung round in a thrust that tore through the musician's jacket. He collapsed.

The small man bent down and quickly rifled through the sax player's clothes, his right hand still clasping the knife. He pocketed something and took off down an alley. I knelt down beside the musician and wiped the mud and rainwater out of his face. He looked up, his mouth twisted with pain.

"I'll get some help—"

Choking, he grabbed my arm. "No police."

"Where's the nearest hospital?"

He shook his head.

"What about the club?"

"No—"

"What the fuck do you want me to do?"

There was no answer.

Bending down, I half-lifted, half-dragged him to his feet. Although we had the same height, he weighed practically nothing. He leaned forward, his hands cupped over his upper chest, his entire body shaking. I held him more tightly.

I saw the man's blood coursing down the front of my leather jacket and onto my hands. I could hear loud voices in the streets behind us, and the word *"Politie!"* shouted repeatedly. You can't get involved in this shit, I thought as I pulled him into the shadows. You realize somebody just tried to kill him!

I knew some basic first aid from my two decades in the tunnels, bandaging and splinting up minor injuries while waiting for help to arrive. There was enough light to see what was going on under the torn fabric, so I leaned him against the wall and carefully pulled the man's bloody fingers away from the wound. Beneath the dirty cloth I found a narrow gash just beside his collarbone. It wasn't anywhere near his heart, and it didn't seem deep, but there was plenty of blood.

I pushed the musician's head back so that his face was visible. And I made a decision.

It must have been near midnight. We were only two blocks from my hotel. I took the man's weight over my shoulder and began to carry him down the passage.

"I don't know why the fuck I'm doing this," I whispered as I took a few more steps with him leaning on my shoulder. "But you better not bleed to death, you piece of shit. . . ."

Fortunately the night clerk was in the rear, the blue light of a television keeping time to his snores. I dragged the sax player through the lobby and into the tiny elevator. The ride to the fifth floor seemed like it wouldn't end, and I had to staunch the blood with my own sleeves so that he wouldn't bleed on the floor. Fumbling with my key, I pulled him straight into the bathroom, sat him on the commode and began peeling away his soiled clothes.

The guy had lost his hat somewhere in the alley. He had a head of wild, thorny hair. His black eyes were teary slits and his purple lips were swollen, but he had my cheekbones and square jaw. I washed the wound with soap and hot water, then soaked a washcloth with cologne and pressed it to the man's chest. The nodding head snapped up in pain, but he made no sound.

I tore up one of my undershirts to make a bandage. Then I half-lifted him to the bed and pulled off the rest of his clothes. He was wearing a faded sweater, a stained cotton shirt, a torn undershirt and filthy pants. There were other bruises on his chest, fading from black to a yellow-edged purple. I yanked off the blackened, toeless socks and nearly gagged at the stench of his underwear.

That's when I saw the purple slashes on his pale inner arms, his neck and his ankles. The marks were fresh. The veins were swollen and red. "Sweet Jesus," I whispered. "You stupid god-damn motherfucker!"

Stumbling into the bathroom, I vomited my stomach empty. When I could stand, I stripped off my own bloody clothes and leaned against the wall of the shower, frantically scrubbing his blood from my body.

When I was dry, I emptied his pockets, then stuffed his ragged clothing into a plastic bag. The man had no money, but I discovered an empty billfold with a dog-eared, yellowed iden-tification card inside. Covering him with a sheet, I took the li-cense back into the bright light of the bathroom to examine it.

The card had a photograph of a Black man, but the shot was so yellow and worn that I could hardly make out the features. The name, almost impossible to read, was Robert Anderson. Birthdate: 1967.

I looked at the man lying on the bed. Either he had changed a lot since that card was issued, or it was somebody else's. I hes-itated—if this really wasn't my brother, then I sure as hell didn't need to have him bleeding all over that hotel room. But if I sent him back into the night, what would happen to him? Was that guy with the knife out there waiting to finish the job? Were the police already looking for both of us? Why was this guy on somebody's hit list anyway?

I took out my own wallet and dug out a slip of paper. Punch-ing the numbers into the phone, I prayed that Elias wouldn't answer.

The phone rang once, twice, three times. Then someone fumbled with the receiver. *"Ja?"* A woman's sleepy voice.

"Sophie? Sophie, it's Abel."

There was a silence. "What time is it?"

"I don't fucking know. Listen, Sophie, I found him. I mean, I think it's him. But someone stabbed him and—"

"What are you talking about?"

"August."

"August?"

"Damn!" I blurted, remembering that she hadn't been with me at the Registry that evening.

"Sophie—I have a brother. The clerk at the Registry said his name is August. You remember what my mother kept saying—"

"A brother?" Her voice grew stronger. "I don't understand."

"I don't either. It looks like my father—well, he was even more of a motherfucker than I realized. The only thing I can tell you now is that I went into that club—you know the one near my hotel—and the guy playing sax—Sophie, I think it's him."

"You think the sax player is your brother? Abel, I—"

"Listen, someone tried to kill him tonight. I have him in my room."

Now the silence on the other end grew troubled. "You should call the police."

"I can't."

"But if he's involved in some kind of shit—"

"I don't want to be the one to turn him in." I struggled for words to explain my feelings. "Look, Sophie, five hours ago I didn't even know that he existed. Now that I might have found him, I can't turn him over to the police. For all I know, I could be giving his life away—"

She exhaled sharply into the phone. "How bad is it?"

"He has a knife wound in his shoulder. I cleaned it and sterilized it and he's not bleeding anymore."

"Bandages?"

"I tore up one of my undershirts."

The man on the bed groaned and I spoke more quickly. "I really need to get him out of here. I understand if you can't help me. But tell me—what the hell should I do?"

There were a few more seconds of silence. Then she spoke. "Try to get him up. I'll be there with a car in twenty minutes."

Twisting an old key in a rusted lock, Sophie threw open the door to a small stone house just a few hundred yards from the sea. I couldn't see very much in the dark, but she lit a hurricane lamp that filled the room with soft light.

Wearing jeans and a hooded sweatshirt, Sophie had pulled up to the hotel about an hour earlier in a compact Renault. Although he had to be in pain, the sax player had managed to walk across the lobby without our help. Fortunately the night clerk was still snoring in the back.

Now I followed Sophie into a kitchen. There wasn't much furniture: a scarred wooden table with four chairs. A gas stove with two burners beside a steel sink. A single peeling white cabinet just beneath the window. And there was a big pile of wood beside a small fireplace.

Sophie opened another door and went inside. Moments afterward a faint light appeared in that room, too. The whole cottage smelled like burned charcoal and the sea.

"The bed is ready," Sophie announced as she came out. "Let's get him inside."

Together we helped the musician from the rear seat of the car and got him into the house. He moved as though he was hurting, but he never spoke. I led him into the small bedroom and helped him onto the narrow bed. Sophie covered him with several woolen blankets that she took from a wardrobe. Within seconds he was asleep.

Taking my arm, she led me back into the kitchen. She began placing paper and twigs in the fireplace.

"The toilet's in there." She nodded toward another door in the corner. "There's no heat, but if you keep a fire burning, you'll both be warm enough." She glanced around. "You'll find rice and some cans of beans in the cabinet. It's too late in the year for most vegetables, but you can look outside when the sun comes up. There might still be some carrots or potatoes growing in the field outside."

She lit the fire and stood up. "There's a cot folded up in that cupboard if you want to sleep."

"He's using, Sophie."

"I can see that. Are you afraid to be alone with him?"

"I can handle it." I paused. "He really does look like my father—"

"Wait until daylight."

"His identification card has a different name—"

"Wait until he can speak."

"And after what my mother was saying—"

"Abel Paulus!" Sophie's tone was sharp. "He's hurt. He needs your help. You'll worry about the rest later."

Suddenly I felt very alone. "Hey," she said softly. "Even if he's not your brother, it's good that you're here with him. I'll be back this evening after my meeting. No one will bother you. If you need a doctor you can go to the house down the road. An old couple lives there. They're good people and will try to help you."

"Where exactly are we?"

"On the coast, about five miles north of Haarlem."

"Who owns this place?"

"I do. It's where I grew up."

With those words she slipped out into the darkness. The sound of her car on the gravel drive was soon replaced by the crackling of the fire. I sat down at the table beside the fireplace and stared into the flames.

The musician started making noise shortly before dawn, calling out for someone. I went into the dim bedroom, my back stiff and sore.

"Hey man," I said, bending down to touch his arm.

He lurched up and grabbed me by the shoulders, pulling me toward him with a surprised cry of pain. I fell forward, landing on his chest. We both cursed and I jerked myself free, grabbing his arms.

"Take it easy, goddammit! You're safe! Do you understand?"

I held him until he quit resisting and laid still on the bed, breathing heavily.

"We're in my friend's house, a few miles outside of Haarlem. Somebody attacked you last night, but you're safe now."

He didn't answer, but there was recognition—and cold distrust—in his eyes. I let go of his arms and he carefully shifted his wounded shoulder.

"You want me to get a doctor?"

He shook his head. I took a little tin from my pocket.

"All I've got is this headache shit I brought from home. You want some?"

He nodded.

"I'll get you some water."

When I returned he was sitting up. His skin was a dull gray in the lamplight. He swallowed the pills, his eyes still fixed on me.

"Here's your wallet." I tossed it on the bed beside him.

"Those rags you had on are in a trash bin in Amsterdam. You're wearing some of my stuff."

"Why?" The word was somewhere between a cough and a snarl.

"Because some asshole tried to kill you."

I waited, but he didn't respond. I crossed the room and opened the shutters.

In the cold gray light we looked like mismatched copies of the same person. We shared skin color and height. But his face was scarred and I could see his scalp through thinning patches of his matted hair. His lips were still swollen from the beat-down he'd taken, but the eyes and nose were Louis's.

I could also see that the sight of me freaked him out.

"Who the fuck are you?" he muttered.

"I told you last night. My name is Abel Crofton. I grew up in New York with my father. When he died last month I decided to come here to try to find my mother."

"And?"

"Turns out she lives in Zandvoort, in a residence for sick people. While I was checking on some family records I discovered I also have a brother."

More silence. I stared at the sax player. He stared back. His face had the look of a half-starved dog.

"Are you August Sebastian Van Gelder?"

"No."

"Okay. Then what *is* your name?"

"Rex."

"Your ID card says Robert Anderson."

"So the fuck what?"

"You look a lot like my father, Louis Crofton. And when you play—man, it's like you're channeling my pops."

The room was silent. A gull cried somewhere outside. The musician closed his eyes. "My name's Rex."

I moved slowly to the doorway. "All right, Rex. You hungry?"

He shook his head.

"I'll get myself some grub."

I was standing at the stove stirring rice in a little saucepan when the musician came out from the back room, shuffling painfully toward the table. His collarbone stuck out from between his stooped shoulders and his legs looked like they might snap just from having to carry his weight. Sinking onto a chair, he hacked up a chestful of phlegm and spat into the fireplace.

"You got a car?"

"No car and no phone. But my friend will be back later on today. You want something to drink?"

"What you got?"

"Water."

"Fuck that. Cigarette?"

I pulled the nearly empty pack from my jacket pocket and tossed it onto the table. Using one hand, the musician flipped open his lighter. He took a puff and began to choke.

"What the fuck is this?"

"What do you mean?"

"The taste—"

"It's menthol."

"Why do you smoke this shit?"

"So assholes like you won't smoke it," I said as I picked up the pack and put it back in my pocket.

He made a noise that was probably meant to be a laugh.

"You from around here?" I asked.

"Yeah. So what?"

"You've got a British accent."

"I lived over there."

"London?"

"Manchester."

"Performing?"

"Sometimes."

I turned off the heat and spooned some rice onto a plate I found in the cabinet. Walking over to the window, I looked outside at the ragged fields. Thin sunlight had broken through the fog. Leaning against the cabinet, I talked as I ate.

"They got any good clubs in Manchester?"

"A few." The musician propped his arm on the tabletop and automatically began running his fingers along the wood, fingering a silent melody.

"You like it better over there?"

"It's different. More brothers. Indians, Arabs, Jamaicans, everything."

"There's a lot of Black people in Amsterdam."

"Not enough."

"Did you play in a band?"

"Yeah."

"Were you any good?"

"Cut some tracks for an album, but we didn't have enough bread to finish it."

"Is that why you left?"

"Why you asking?"

"Just curious."

I came back and sat down across from him at the table. Even though I'd managed to wash his face and chest the night before, the kitchen stank of alcohol and sweat.

"So you got any family?"

"Who gives a fuck?"

His cracked lips opened and he stared into the fire. His nostrils flared as he breathed out a long stream of smoke. There was something beautiful about his scarred face, which carried even more pain than my father's.

"You know," I said, "I never knew my mother. I acted like I didn't give a shit when I was a kid. But it started to get to me when I got older. I couldn't figure out why she never came looking for me. I thought that she was out there somewhere, having a good life, maybe even with a new family. That shit really fucked me up."

"What about your father?"

"Let's just say we weren't too close."

"Why not?"

"He never did shit with his life. Never lived anyplace decent or managed to make it work with a woman."

"You got money?"

"No. I lay cables for the Manhattan Power Company."

"You got a house?"

"No—a little apartment."

"Wife?"

"No."

"You don't sound too different from your father."

Fuck you, I thought. He smiled like he knew what I was thinking.

"You a *pouf*?" he asked.

"A what?"

"A fag."

"No, asshole. I'm the idiot who saved your goddamned life."

"That was fucking stupid." He laughed again. "You live in New York?"

"I live in Harlem."

I saw a flicker of real interest cross his face.

"Your Haarlem seems to be a pretty nice town," I said, "but it's a lot different from my Harlem."

"How?"

"My Harlem isn't a city. It's a world." I lit a cigarette and leaned forward, resting my arms on the table.

"My Harlem has its own artists. Poets. Musicians. The best jazz in the world. I know you heard about the Apollo. Everybody who matters in Black music has played there, though personally I prefer the smaller clubs. Like the place where you played last night. I like to head on up to the Lenox Lounge late nights when I'm not working. That's where you can get some real face time with the musicians.

"We folks in Harlem have our own way of doing things. A whole different way of life. Take, for instance, the way people try to sell stuff in Amsterdam. I mean, those sidewalk pancakes look good and all, but you ain't lived until you smelled the ribs grilling outside of Nina's Place on Broadway. And the folks in my Harlem are always thinking up some new shit to sell you while the sidewalk preachers are trying to save your soul. And the women—" I whistled, "you don't got dick enough for all them fine sisters."

"You talk like it's some kind of paradise."

"Paradise is one thing for white men: big houses, big cars, big bank accounts. But when you're Black, it's something different."

There was a long silence.

"You said your father played music?"

"Sax. Like you."

"Famous?"

"Could've been if he hadn't been drunk every day of his life."

"And you?"

"Can't play a note. But I haven't had a drink for twelve years."

"Why the hell not?"

"Because my life was shit when I was drinking."

"Life is shit, anyway."

"Not always."

"Always," he said with a dry laugh. "I grew up with some-body who hates music. All she wanted was for me to go to school and be a goddamn teacher. But I hated that bloody bor-ing shit. I cut out of there as soon as I could."

"So you've been playing a long time?"

"All my fucking life. I never had a teacher or nothing. I was born to do this shit. It's in my blood."

"You ever been married?"

He reached up and scratched his matted hair. "There was this one sister from Jamaica. Nelda. We was living together in Man-chester. But after a while she started going on about me fixing cars or washing windows or some bloody shit. All of them the same."

"I'm feeling you on that." I paused. "How long you been on the needle?"

"Why do you care?"

"I was thirteen when I took my first drink. I had never felt anything so good in my life. It was like my whole world opened up: I was warm, happy and had everything I needed. Even the most dangerous motherfucker on the street couldn't scare me. It made me feel like a man."

"I don't need to take no shit to feel like a man," he answered. "But it opens me up to my music. I tried all the shit that's out there, but nothing else does it."

"Did you ever try to quit?"

"I don't want to quit."

"Excuse me, but you don't look so good. And that dude last night wasn't trying to make you look any better."

He laughed again. "Who gives a shit if I live one day or twenty years?"

"Maybe your brother would."

"What could a brother do for me?"

"He could help you get to New York."

"There ain't nothing for me in New York."

"There's Harlem."

"I can't go there."

"Why not? Planes don't cost that much."

"I still need papers and all that other shit."

"With an American brother, you could probably live in the States. Of course, you couldn't be involved in anything illegal."

"So you're going to take your brother to America?"

"First I have to find him. Then I have to make sure he's not doing any stupid shit that might fuck up his life—or mine."

"And if he don't pass your test? You go back to your Harlem and he stays here?"

"That depends on whether he's willing to change."

"You mean, if he's willing to be like you?"

"I don't know."

"There's too damn much you don't know."

The short day had already drifted into darkness when Sophie's car ground its way up the gravel drive. The musician had vanished into the bedroom hours before, so I went out into the twilight to meet her.

She was leaning over the trunk in a heavy sweater and tight-fitting jeans, trying to lift a large box from the rear seat. I took it from her arms.

"Shit—this is heavy."

"I brought you some food. And a couple of blankets and a change of clothes."

"How did you—" I glanced into the box and found some sweatpants and a package of new T-shirts.

"I guessed. He's the same height as you."

The fire had nearly burned out in the kitchen. "Put some more wood on," she said with a glance at the grate. "It'll be cold in here soon."

Seeing that the musician was asleep, I closed the bedroom door and knelt down beside the fireplace. Sophie was standing at the table, emptying the box. The firelight made her even more beautiful.

"So what's he like?"

"Tough as hell."

"What did you tell him, Abel?"

"The truth."

"He believed you?"

"Maybe. But he sure as hell doesn't trust me."

"I've seen him around, you know. Sometimes alone. Other times with street dealers. He's been playing at that club for a while, but I never go in there because . . ." She gazed down into the empty box. "Are you sure you're right about him?"

"No. But he looks and acts so much like my father."

"And you really want him to be your brother." She sighed and raised her head, smoothing her wild hair away from her eyes. "If he won't admit that he's related to you, what are you going to do? This man is in trouble. He's still using, and people are trying to hurt him. He could bring you a lot of difficulty."

"But if I walk away without knowing, why the hell did I come here?"

"You found your mother."

"But she can't tell me anything."

"I'll go back to the residence with you. Perhaps if we keep talking to her—"

"She wanted me to find him, Sophie. That's why she kept saying his name."

"Maybe she just wants to know where he is, or whether he's still alive."

"And if he really is my brother?"

"This man is not capable of caring about you. He's hurt. From the looks of things, he's homeless. And it won't be long before he needs that shit in his system. Are you willing to deal with that?"

"You think we should drive back to Amsterdam and just dump him in the street?"

"Maybe he'll talk to me."

I laughed softly. "It's crazy, isn't it? I traveled halfway around the world to find some trace of my family, and he's doing everything he can to throw his away."

She went to the sink, reaching to the bottom of the cabinet to pull out a heavy iron skillet. "I'll make you some eggs—"

"Damn," I said, suddenly ashamed of myself. "Look, Sophie—I'll cook. Sit down and let me take care of it."

Sophie sank into the chair with a grateful sigh. I lit the gas with a match and set the pan on the fire. Glancing over my shoulder I found her staring at the stone floor.

"It's funny," she said as she lit a cigarette. "When I was a child my little sister used to chase me around this table with the broom, screaming 'I'll sweep your feet and you'll never fall in love!' "

"I guess she never caught you."

"She caught me every day."

"What about your husband?"

"What about him?"

"Doesn't sound like a happy marriage."

"It keeps him amused."

"And how does it keep you?"

"Not all people marry for love. Particularly women. Some of us marry for money. Or for safety."

I cracked six eggs into the skillet and tossed in a chunk of butter. "Then why did you sleep with me?"

"It just happened."

"Shit like that doesn't just happen."

"Of course it does. You have to accept that, Abel."

"Because I can't change it?"

"Because it's who I am."

"What the fuck does that mean?"

"Do you really want to know?" she asked, her eyes never leaving my face. "I was born here, in this room, on a bed that used to be pushed into that corner." She nodded toward an empty space by the rough plaster wall.

"My parents came here from Suriname, Dutch Guyana. My father's grandparents were coolies from East Asia. My mother's grandparents were African slaves.

"You asked me once if I'm really Dutch. Well, in truth I'm both Indian and African. Yet even with all that history, all that culture, my father and mother had nothing more than these two rooms to give their four children."

"Four children?"

"Yes. Two boys and two girls. All six of us living together in this little house, with my father trying to scratch enough potatoes from that field to keep us from starving. It was quite a childhood."

"Are your parents still alive?"

"No."

"How'd you get to Amsterdam?"

"The way most girls do. With a man I met in a bar."

"A boyfriend?"

"A pimp."

I forgot the eggs until I smelled them burning. I flicked off the gas and moved the pan to another burner. "Did you—I mean, you weren't—"

"Yes. I was a prostitute. And a junkie, too. With my own picture window and a bed that was big enough for three or four, if the price was right. You asked me how I learned such good English? Well, you'd be impressed by the united nations I serviced—"

We both looked up to find the musician leaning in the bedroom doorway.

"I want to go. Now."

"I'm making food," I said quietly. "First you should eat something."

"No food." He moved forward, his eyes fixed on Sophie.

She said something in Dutch and he halted, his body wavering drunkenly.

"What the hell did you say to him?"

"I told him I have what he needs."

"You *what*?"

"It's outside."

I opened my mouth in surprise, but was stopped by her icy look. She stood up and glanced at Rex, whose sunken eyes were like empty holes.

"I'll be right back."

I caught her outside the house as she returned from the car with a plastic packet.

"What the fuck is that?"

"It's methadone."

"Where did you get it?"

"That doesn't matter—"

"Is that shit legal?"

"Look"—she took my arm firmly—"you want him to trust you? You want him to tell you who he is?"

"Not while he's high!"

"He's not going to tell you anything while he's vomiting his guts out! If he gets sick we'll have to take him to a hospital. The hospital will contact the police because of that hole in his chest. And if the police are looking for him—"

"All right!" I shouted, jerking my arm free. "But all this makes me sick. Do you understand?"

For a moment neither of us spoke. Then she slipped past me and went into the house. Pissed off as hell, I stared into the night.

I don't know how long I stood there. Suddenly Sophie called out from the doorway and I went inside. There was no sign of the musician.

"Come in and close the door," she said from the stove. "You're letting in the cold."

My eyes swept the table, which was now set for two. The kitchen was warm with the smell of fried eggs, hot coffee and toasting bread.

"Where did you get it? Does Elias keep a little stash in the medicine chest in case you have some junkie friends over for dinner?"

She paused, then turned off the gas. "Do you want to eat?"

"I'm still waiting for an answer."

"He's an addict, Abel. He can't function without it."

"But I'm not going to help him get high—"

"Then you have to take him back to the same place you found him. You have no right to keep him here against his will."

We ate without speaking, then Sophie leaned back in her chair and looked into the fire. Her face seemed to soften, like when we were on the train. She glanced over at me and our eyes locked. I had a sudden aching memory of her warm, sweet flesh and I wondered for the first time if I had pleased her when we had sex.

"Sophie, I want you to tell me everything."

"Are you sure?"

"Go ahead."

She shrugged, turning back to the fireplace. "Well, there wasn't much to eat. My father drank, and when he was drunk he beat my mother. So she drank, too, and hit my brothers. And then they hit my sister and me."

"Nobody gave a shit? Your teachers—"

"Tried hard to turn us into nice little white children. But we were just too different. My parents preferred curry and salt fish to potatoes and cheese. We had no money for clothes, books or religious classes. I remember how the other children teased us because we didn't make our first communion."

She looked toward the dark window.

"This time of year the Dutch have a tradition. Some people dress up in robes like Black Peter, the monk who helped Saint Niklaus deliver food to the poor. They go through the streets, giving candy and toys to the children.

"My father always volunteered to do this so he could bring a little extra money—and some sweets—back home to us. But afterward, the other kids made fun of us, saying that my father couldn't wash the black off his face. They said our skin was dirty, too. And that we were ugly and poor, like the children in Africa."

"Didn't someone try to stop them?"

"We weren't important enough. And my father thought that if he made trouble we might be driven from this house. He believed this was the best he could do."

"So what happened?"

"When I got a bit older I was sent to a trade school to learn to be a cook. I lived at a special house for girls. At night we all went out to the bars. There were often people who came to the town for the weekend. I met Klaus, a German who was living in Amsterdam.

"Klaus told me the night we met that I was beautiful. He told me I was throwing my life away in that kitchen. He promised he'd give me something better. He was the first person who ever said things like that to me. So when he asked me to leave with him, I was happy to go."

"How old were you?"

"Fifteen."

"Didn't your parents—"

"No. He told me to write to them and tell them that I was going to Amsterdam to become a clerk in a big store. I told them that I would earn good money and have a nice place to live. He gave me some cash to send to them so they wouldn't try to stop me."

She lit another cigarette and stared into the fire.

"At first he was good to me. He bought me nice clothes and took me to restaurants and the theater. He told me I had a beautiful body. Like any young girl, I was willing to do anything to please him.

"And then one night he was drinking and getting high with

a friend. I wanted to show them how grown up I was, so I got high, too. When his friend took me into the bedroom, I hardly realized what was happening. When it was over I was afraid Klaus would be angry. But instead, he told me he was proud of me, and that I had made him very happy."

She drew her small foot back and forth across the stone floor.

"After that, I got high all the time. Klaus shared me with many of his friends. Then he took me into that part of the city and showed me the girls in the windows. He said that I would make a lot of money for us if I would do that. And so I did."

She lifted her cigarette to her lips, inhaled and blew the smoke over the table.

"I had my regulars—people who traveled from England and Germany once or twice a month to be with me. You would be amazed how much some of them come to depend on you. As if those nights gave them something to look forward to and dream about during their normal lives."

There was a stirring in the other room. Sophie walked over and looked inside. She then closed the door softly and returned to the table.

"The fucked-up thing is that I had to be high to do it. I often wonder if I could have survived without the drugs. But it's as if you don't exist anymore. You're not attached to your flesh. You don't have any will, hope or personal desires. You only exist to please others."

"How long were you in?"

"Ten years."

"How did you get out?"

"Somebody finally made me believe that I deserved better. So I went to a clinic and signed myself in. It took me over a year to get my life together. And then I met Elias."

"Does he love you?"

"He thinks he's protecting me, though I've survived more than he can ever imagine."

"Are you happy with him?"

"Marriage isn't like the movies. A man and a woman don't meet, look into each other's eyes and spend the rest of their lives together."

"They could if they really loved each other."

"What do you know about love?"

She stood up and walked to the sink. She began washing the dishes, her back to me. For a long time neither of us spoke.

"Abel, what made you stop drinking?"

"Like most people, something happened that made me wake up."

"What was it?"

"Sophie, I—"

"Tell me, Abel."

"Well, I came to one morning and I didn't know where the fuck I was. I had no idea how I got there or what the hell I had done.

"The room was jet-black and I was naked. I was still so drunk that my head was rolling and I knew I was going to puke if I didn't get outside, but I couldn't find my clothes. While I was feeling around for my pants my hand touched somebody's face. Shit—I was off that mattress so fast you would have thought that somebody poured gas on it and lit a match.

"When I hit the floor I made a lot of noise and a man started yelling from some other room. Then the door opened and there I was, staring into the face of a little kid. She started screaming and the woman on the bed sat up and started yelling at her to shut up. Another door opened and a man started coming down the hall.

"I found my shit and managed to get some of it on while I

was gagging my way out onto the fire escape. I made it to the lowest level, then jumped down to the street and landed on an overturned garbage can. The smell of all that rotting shit made me start puking all over myself. I just kind of folded up on the curb, next to a dead rat, covered in vomit.

"Then I heard this voice: A young chick was standing there beside me in nothing but her panties and a T-shirt, with that little kid balanced on her hip. She held out my wallet, opened it and took out a fifty, then threw it in the gutter. I swear she was only about fifteen.

"I crawled to my feet, dragged myself to the corner and tried to figure out where the hell I was. I had landed on my ankle and it felt like it was broken, but my cash was gone and nobody was going to pick me up stinking like that. So I just started doing my best imitation of walking. It took me about four hours to stagger my way through the city streets, all the way back to my crib.

"I had finally hit my bottom. I knew that the only thing left for me was to end up in some other room where somebody would kill me. I just got lucky that time."

Sophie turned off the water and faced me. "So you're alone because you blame women for your addiction."

"What?"

"You believe that your mother abandoned you and all the rest of us just want to use you. You feel much safer when you're not close to anyone."

"I'm alone because I've never met a woman who wasn't a bitch."

"Most of us have to be."

There was a tense silence.

"Abel," she said quietly, "why don't you lie down for a while?"

I pulled the cot out of the cupboard and unfolded it. I stretched out and turned on my side, pulling one of the blankets up over my shoulders. Sophie went and sat down by the fire.

We were so close. We were so far apart. I wanted her with all my heart, and feared her more than I'd ever feared anyone.

Even Louis.

One of the toughest things I ever did was to refuse to let Louis move in with me.

He'd been in the workhouse, serving time for taking some money out of the cashbox at a bar where he was playing. He told the cops he was just collecting his pay. The owner said his pay went down in double bourbons before, during and after his performance.

His parole officer told him he needed to stay off the streets. So the asshole told his p.o. he was coming to live with me.

I was surprised when they showed up at my crib one afternoon: this worn-out, faded old man in some Salvation Army rags about two sizes too big. And a young, still wet-behind-the-ears white cat from Jersey. I hadn't seen Louis for about six months and I was shocked at how beat-up he looked. They sat down in my living room and right away my father asked for a drink. I told him I wasn't drinking anymore.

"What the hell do you mean by that—not drinking anymore? What the fuck is wrong with you?"

"I quit, Pop."

"There's nothing wrong with a shot of liquor every once in a while."

I turned to the white guy.

"What's he supposed to do to make things right with the court?"

"Obviously he has to stay out of trouble. I'm sure you're aware of your father's history of arrests for public drunkenness and disorderly conduct. If he gets picked up again the feds will take over."

"The motherfucker didn't pay me and I took what was mine," Louis said as he lit up one of my cigarettes.

"We'd really like to see him get into a court-ordered rehab," the p.o. continued, "but unfortunately the judge didn't order it."

"I don't need no fucking rehab. I can stop drinking whenever I want."

"What am I supposed to do with him?" I asked the officer. "I can't make him do shit."

"We figure that if he has somewhere to go and someone to come home to it might keep him out of trouble."

"It never did before," I answered. My father had stood up and was walking through my place, searching for liquor.

"Mr. Crofton's getting up in age and will soon need somebody to look after him."

I glanced across the room at my father. I knew I was supposed to feel some kind of duty, or respect, or even pity for him. But I didn't.

"Listen, I'm afraid I can't help out with this. My place is too small and I work too much to keep him out of trouble."

"You don't have to keep me nowhere," Louis said loudly. "I just need a place to crash till I get a few gigs and get back on my feet."

"That might take months and as long as you're drinking I don't want you around."

"When the fuck did you decide you're too good to be around me?"

"When I decided to get clean."

"Listen, you punk motherfucker—I fed you and clothed you and gave you a place to sleep all of your childhood—"

"And I ended up a drunk, just like you. That's got to stop, Pop. I just can't live like that no more."

"You ain't shit now and you ain't never gonna be shit. You think that because you can refuse a drink you can walk away from your father? Listen, asshole—"

It was the p.o. who got up and took my father's arm. He led Louis away as the old man went on shouting insults. The p.o. stopped at the door.

"I'll find him somewhere else to stay." He paused, looked into my face. "How long?"

"Twelve weeks," I said.

"Good for you, buddy. And don't feel bad. You made the right call today."

I was out cold, dreaming some shit about a glass room filled with tulips. My pockets were full of plane-sized bottles and I opened them one at a time, taking a good sip of the bourbon before pouring it on the flowers as a libation for my father.

I woke up to Sophie's voice. She was sitting with the musician at the table a few feet away.

"Oh, look," he said. "Brother Man is coming back from the dead."

"Taking care of you is enough to kill anybody."

The room smelled of coffee and warm bread.

"It's five in the morning," Sophie said. "I've got to be back to open Vetiver's before seven."

I sat up. I needed fresh air and I needed to piss. The musician was still grinning in my direction. He was still fucked up.

"Rex wants to come back to the city," Sophie said. "So I guess you'll be coming, too."

"But—"

"We have to go back, Abel."

"Didn't you say you live in Haarlem?" I asked the musician.

"I live wherever the fuck I want."

The trip back to Amsterdam was tense. It was still dark when we pulled up in front of Central Station. As Rex opened the car door I reached out and took his arm.

"How do I find you?"

"Let it go, man."

"Will you be back at the club tonight?"

"I don't know."

"Are you going to be safe?"

"Never."

"Look—you can't just disappear."

"Why the fuck not?"

"What if that asshole comes after you?"

"That's my fucking problem."

"What if I'm right? What if we are brothers?"

"I don't give a shit."

He slammed the door and walked away, favoring his shoulder. Sophie put the car into gear and drove the few blocks to my hotel. At the entrance she turned off the motor.

"Are you going to tell your mother about this?"

"What fucking difference does it make? There's nothing she can do."

"She deserves to know."

"What? That I picked up some junkie asshole and invited him into the family?"

"She's worried about him—"

"That's not my problem."

Sophie shook her head. "Oh—I see. You don't want to talk to her because you're angry. Being with him brought back all that shit you felt about her abandoning you."

"I have a right to be pissed off."

"And she has the right to explain herself."

I looked at Sophie for a long moment. Forcing the frustration out of my voice, I made myself speak softly.

"Will Elias be angry because you didn't come home last night?"

"No. He'll figure I was with my sister."

"Your sister lives in Amsterdam?"

"Maybe you saw her when you walked through the city the other night, looking very beautiful in her very own window."

"You're telling me—"

"She followed me to Amsterdam sixteen years ago. She even worked with me for a while."

"Sweet Jesus, woman!"

Sophie laughed, but her eyes were suddenly shining. "I'm trying, Abel. I've got her halfway there, but I just can't seem to make the rest happen."

"What do you mean?"

"I helped her get clean nine months ago. Now I've got her into a program. That's why I have to go to the meetings every day. She counts on me being there with her. But—you see, she's not completely out of the other thing yet. There's a man who— well, sometimes I stay with her at night. It keeps her off the streets."

"That's where you went when you left my room?"

"Yes."

"And Elias knows—"

"Of course."

"And your brothers?"

"They left the country years ago."

"So you're doing this alone."

"I'm doing it alone."

I didn't know what to say or do. So we sat there for a while without speaking. Then she looked at her watch and turned the key in the ignition. "I've got to get to work."

She drove away and I stood there on the street, hungry, tired and strangely sad.

I was about three months off the bottle when Serge stopped me as we left a meeting.

"Got something for you, Abe." He pulled a worn paperback from a bag and shot that white boy grin at me.

I looked at the book's cover—a Black cowboy, complete with leather pants and gleaming spurs, was reining in a rearing white horse while a bunch of impressed-looking Indians stood around watching.

"What the hell is this?"

"It's a book. You open it up and read it."

"I don't have time for this shit."

"Sure you do. You read it while you're on the train and while you're on your lunch break—or whatever you do at four in the morning—and while you're sitting on the can."

"But why would I read this crap?"

"Because it's crap. It'll take your mind off liquor."

"I'd rather be thinking about something warm and wet—"

"Who knows? Maybe there's some of that in this book."

"I don't need you going out and buying books for me."

"I didn't buy this for you. I bought it for myself. I finished it yesterday and I want somebody else to read it so we can talk about it."

"You don't read this shit, man. You're a teacher."

"I'll read anything that helps me forget about booze for a while."

"But this is stupid shit."

"That's right, buddy. I want you to read it so we can talk about what stupid shit it is!"

I was ashamed to admit to Serge that in my thirty-three years on earth I'd never read an adult book. Back in the Dr. Seuss days my teachers tried their best, but it was damn near impossible to teach me anything. What with Louis coming in at all hours of the night, often so drunk that he couldn't see straight, my world was always crazy. I finally left school in the ninth grade, and in all the years I'd been drinking I'd never so much as looked at a newspaper.

Serge patted me on the back. "After you finish this one you can come with me to that used bookstore down on West Nineteenth and we'll try to find something that's more suited to your exceptional literary taste."

"Why?"

"Because I'm sick of talking about nothing but pussy and booze. Come on, Abe—let's expand our intellectual horizons."

"This book isn't going to expand shit."

"Well, until I've found something more to your taste, this will have to do."

I would never tell Serge how I struggled with that book. How I threw it in a corner after realizing I could barely make it through the first paragraph. How I avoided looking at the torn cover for days. How I finally sounded out the longer words, saying them aloud like a first-grader. And how proud I was, when almost three months after he'd given it to me, I sat down in our favorite diner to discuss it with him. Over those three months I had come to believe that that pathetic book was the greatest piece of literature ever written. I could hardly express my pride in having worked my way through every single word.

And true to his word, we left the diner and strolled down to that bookstore, where Serge helped me pick out another novel. A few weeks later we went back and chose another. Over time I came to love Chester Himes and Ishmael Reed, James Baldwin and the great Du Bois. I learned about our history from Lerone Bennett and Carter G. Woodson. I even memorized some Paul Laurence Dunbar and Langston Hughes.

Most of all, I read every book about alcoholism I could get my hands on. I spent hours talking with Serge about the shit I was learning. About how drugs and liquor stop too many brothers before they even get started. And I thought a lot about how few of us ever get to tell our stories.

That's why I decided that one day I would write my story. But I would have to stay alive—and sober—to do it.

At five-fifteen I was standing outside the stone building across from the Registry. What I was doing there, I don't know. Even if I found the meeting, I sure as hell wouldn't understand a word of what they were saying. And I didn't want to give Sophie the vibe that I was stalking her. I mean, it looked like I couldn't get through one single day without seeing her.

But the truth was that I was lost. Everything I'd learned in my recovery told me that I had to find a way to reconcile what was going on between me and the man who might be my brother. It was hard for me to admit that I didn't have the will—and I sure as hell didn't know the way to make that happen. Then I thought about Sophie and her sister. And I figured that checking them out together might help.

A young dude rode up on a motor scooter and parked it beside a bicycle rack.

"Excuse me. I'm looking for a meeting. Do you know where it is?"

He shook his head and answered in Dutch.

I tried Cave Man. "Meeting? Here? Five-thirty?"

"Ah, ontmoeting!" He reached into his pocket and brought out a palm-sized volume—a book of meditations on sobriety.

"Yes. That's it."

"Come," the man replied, motioning for me to follow him.

The meeting was in a small room with a circle of chairs that were nearly full. Like the meetings I attended in New York, the group was made up of all kinds of people. I saw suits, backpacks and even knitting needles.

I stood in the rear, looking for Sophie. Just before five-thirty she showed up, out of breath and windblown.

She scanned the room. Not seeing her sister in the circle, she seemed ready to leave when a movement in the corner stopped her short.

I wouldn't have taken them for family. They shared skin tones, but the sister had a comic-book body. Big thighs, big tits and no waist. She had on a '70s-style apple hat with the brim pulled low, but bleached blond hair cascaded down her back. Then came the fake leather jacket and the spandex tights. She looked like a contestant on the "I Wanna Be a New York Ho" show.

Sophie went to the back of the room and tried to hug her. But the sister pulled away, sat down on the floor and drew her knees up to her forehead.

The meeting began with the group reciting together. I could follow some of it because it was just like my meetings at home.

Then some people got up to share. The circle greeted them and I tried to decipher at least some of the stuff. I mean, you can usually tell how long somebody's been straight by the level of stress in their voice and body language. I thought back to my early days, when every hour without alcohol seemed like an eternity. Back when the Serenity Prayer was my mantra. When I had to close my eyes to walk past the bars on Adam Clayton Powell. And I remembered how much safer I felt when I was surrounded by other folks who were fighting to stay sober.

Someone stood up and offered me a chair, so I joined the group. This was straight out of Serge's fantasies: the chance to meet some folks who might discuss the liberalization of drug laws or the success of needle-exchange programs in Holland. As for me, I just sat back and enjoyed the positive energy of the fellowship.

When the meeting ended many of the people came up and welcomed me in English. It took me a few minutes to get over to Sophie, who seemed okay with my showing up like that.

"Saskia," she said as she took her sister's arm, "this is my friend who lives in America."

"Nice to meet you, Saskia."

Sophie's sister raised her head.

There it was: the Hunger. Without some shit in her system her entire world had been stripped raw. She turned away and I saw that a bruise darkened the entire left side of her face. Her body may have been clean, but her soul was still in the street.

She didn't speak.

"Abel," Sophie said, "I'm going to walk Saskia home. You want to join us?"

We went out into the night. Sophie talked about the folks who had come into the café that day. Saskia walked beside her like a spike-heeled robot. It reminded me of a night twelve years before, when I was doing my own imitation of a zombie as I walked with Serge:

"This shit is killing me, man. It's been *two* fucking months and I don't think I'm gonna make it—"

"Just take it one day at a time, Abe. Or maybe one hour. Or just concentrate on getting through this conversation."

"Saskia and I are thinking about taking the train down to Paris for the New Year," Sophie was saying.

Saskia looked into the entrance of a bar as we passed. A man standing near the door called out to her. I saw Sophie's grip on her sister's arm tighten. I remembered when Serge had taken my arm, too, to steady me.

I was pulled back to reality by the sound of Sophie speaking in Dutch to her sister. We had stopped in front of a narrow row house with a small travel agency on the ground floor. Posters of Venice were taped to the windows. Saskia hesitated at the entrance, then raised her eyes to the dark windows on the top floor.

"Go on up," Sophie said to her in English. "I'll come back later."

"You don't have to. I'll be all right." It was the first time she'd spoken. Her voice was like cut glass. We watched as she unlocked the door and went inside.

"She's lucky to have you," I said to Sophie.

"I don't know about that."

"I do." I didn't wait for her to reply. Taking her into my arms, I kissed her. Right there, in the middle of the street.

After a few seconds she gently pushed me away. "Abel, we have to—"

I kissed her again.

"Abel—"

"Come on, baby. You know you can do better than that."

This time her mouth opened and her tongue found mine. I felt her body loosen up in my arms.

"Now that was pretty good," I said. "But we really need to give it a lot more practice."

She didn't want to laugh, but she did anyway. The sound was nice.

"It's just past seven," I said. "You think my mother's still awake?"

She smiled. "Let's go find out."

We stopped by Sophie's so she could get a warmer jacket. The door opened as she was searching for her key, and there was Elias, a cigarette in one hand, a wineglass in the other.

Sophie said something in Dutch and he bowed like he was the butler.

I followed Sophie into the apartment and Elias closed the door behind us.

"Sit down, Abel," she said as she vanished down a darkened corridor. "I'll be right back."

Elias led me into a room with a low ceiling and windows that looked out over the canal. Dark wooden beams crossed the roof and walls. Most of the furniture looked like it was old and expensive. I sat on a black leather sofa that faced a painting of a naked woman.

"May I get you something to drink? Some coffee, or a glass of wine?"

"No thanks. We'll only be here a minute."

"So you're off on another adventure?"

"I don't know what Sophie's told you, but—"

"Everything, I expect. She's never wasted much time on unnecessary lies."

He sat on the arm of a steel-framed chair and flicked his ashes into a heavy glass ashtray.

"My wife is helping you with some family matters."

"That's right."

"Sophie loves helping others. She's really quite a Samaritan. I suspect that it has to do with her culture—the idea of the extended kinship and all."

"I thought Sophie was Dutch."

"Her parents were colonials, of course. They often live very differently from average Dutch people."

"Do they?" I wasn't even trying to hide the fact that I thought he was an asshole. He wasn't being shy about his feelings, either.

"Tell me, friend, has Sophie told you how we met?"

"No."

"I was the director of the halfway house where she lived when she left the clinic."

I must have looked surprised, because Elias smiled. "Afterward I left my job and opened Vetiver's. I wanted to help her escape her past. I thought that if we could work together, in a way that would keep us very close, she would have a chance to build a new life."

"I guess that makes you quite a Samaritan, too."

He laughed coldly and drew hard on his cigarette. "Sophie tells me you are also in recovery."

"That's right."

"How long?"

"Twelve years, give or take a few weeks."

"Congratulations. That is quite an accomplishment. I suppose that being such an expert on sobriety, you understand the problem with a woman like Sophie."

"Problem?"

"People who begin using at a very early age never experience normal emotional development. They have a great deal of trouble taking on adult responsibilities and forming permanent relationships."

"Isn't she married to you?"

He laughed again. "You know, when I was a little boy I was obsessed with a cat that lived in the streets. She was a big gray cat with long hair and orange eyes. She was as elegant as a panther and so fierce that the dogs were afraid of her. I wanted her to be mine so badly that I left food out for her every day. And every day I'd come back, and the food was gone. It took me a long time to understand that I wasn't actually in love with her. I was in love with the idea of capturing her. And, of course, I never did."

"I guess you didn't learn your lesson."

"To tell you the truth," he said in a light voice, "I really didn't want to."

Sophie came into the room. She was dressed in a fur-lined coat, dark pants, and had a small leather satchel over her shoulder.

"Are you going to Saskia's?" Elias asked, still trying to sound unconcerned.

She said something in Dutch and opened the door. "Come on, Abel. I'm sure you've heard enough."

I crossed the room, feeling Elias's eyes on my back. When I got to the threshold I couldn't stop myself from looking back. He turned away like he didn't give a shit that I was leaving with his wife.

"So is this just a game the two of you play?" I asked her as we went down the stairs. "You bring men home and he pretends not to care."

"The only thing he cares about is himself."

"He said he opened the café for you."

"Did he?"

I took her arm, forcing her to stop one step below me.

"Is it true that you met in a halfway house?"

She looked up at me. "Elias was a rich boy who went into social services to make himself feel better about his privileges. The minute his father died he took his inheritance and opened Vetiver's—and not for me, I promise you."

"Do you love him?"

"Does it matter?"

"It does to me."

"Why, Abel? You don't have relationships with women. You just sleep with them. You came here to find your mother, not someone to love. So don't lie to me—or to yourself—about what's going on between us."

"You're lying to your husband—"

"That's between the two of us."

"I'd say it's between the three of us."

"Elias is not important to me right now. My first duty is to my sister."

"What about me?"

"You're leaving for New York in about five days."

"You could come, too."

"You need to respect the fact that I have a life here."

"I could make you happy—"

"This isn't about happiness. It's about doing what's right."

"Then why are you cheating on your husband?"

"It really doesn't matter. He's already sleeping with Galine."

For the first time the nurse led us directly to a residential wing.

"Frau Van Gelder is doing much better this evening," she said as she knocked on the door to my mother's apartment. "But please remember that she tires very quickly."

My mother had a nice place: a little sofa with two matching armchairs, a couple of landscapes on the wall and some roses on a sideboard loaded with photographs. I could see the corner of a bed in a connecting room. She was dozing on a recliner facing a small television.

"Frau Van Gelder?" Sophie said softly.

My mother opened her eyes and looked from Sophie to me. Her face burst into its crooked smile. She held out her good hand.

I wasn't sure what to do, but she grabbed my wrist and pulled me into her arms.

I don't believe in Kodak moments. But something crazy happened when she hugged me. It was like that feeling you get when a glass of scotch rides you high above your pain—the kind of wrapped-in-a-blanket sensation that all drunks love.

But it was something else, too: for a minute it was like I had never done anything wrong or stupid or mean in my life.

After a while I got myself together and pulled one of those chairs up right beside her. Sophie sat across from us on the edge of the sofa.

"Please, Sophie," I said. "Tell her I'm sorry I couldn't come yesterday."

Sophie spoke slowly to Justina, who nodded shakily.

"Tell her—tell her I know I have a brother named August."

Sophie spoke to Justina, who answered in broken syllables.

"She asked where he is."

"She doesn't know where he's living?"

"No. But she's worried about him." Sophie began to talk in Dutch real slow. The old woman's eyes moved to the sideboard. She said a few words and Sophie got up, returning with a small gold-framed photo.

"This is the only picture she has here of your brother."

A boy looked back at me with quiet eyes and a self-conscious smile. He had clear, coffee-and-cream skin and short curly hair. There wasn't much Abel in his face. But there was a lot of Louis.

And yes, even though booze and smack had fucked him up good, it was obvious that this was the sax player as a kid.

My mother spoke again.

"She says that August is the same as his father."

"The same as Louis?"

"Yes—the alcohol and drugs."

"When was the last time she saw him?"

Sophie put the question to my mother, who looked at me as she answered.

"Two years ago."

I stood up slowly. Justina reached up and grasped my hand like she was scared I would leave. Then she pushed a few more sentences out.

"Abel, your mother says she's sorry."

"What?"

"She's sorry that you had to grow up without her."

My mother started shaking her head, the movement growing more intense as her eyes again filled with tears. She began to speak, the words bubbling through an uncontrollable flow of saliva from the slack side of her mouth. She tried to clean her lips with the handkerchief, but she didn't want to let go of my hand.

I sat down when I saw the troubled expression on Sophie's face. She leaned closer to my mother and asked her more questions. It took a while for her to get her answers out.

"Okay. Let me see if I can get this straight. Your mother says she was only twenty or so when her parents died. She left Haarlem to find work in Amsterdam. She met your father in a club. He was still a soldier. He came to stay with her whenever he had leave. Then, when he was discharged they got married.

"She says things were never good between them. She wanted him to work, but he only wanted to make music. When you and August were born, things got worse.

"He started drinking, and he beat her when he was drunk. One day, while he was playing in another city, your mother took you and August and moved back to her parents' house in Haarlem. When Louis returned and couldn't find you he went crazy. He had a fight with a man who lived in the building, and the man died. Then he went looking for her."

I turned to my mother. Her eyes were closed tight.

"He found her, of course. He told her he was going back to America. He wanted her to come with him."

"To New York?"

"Yes. But she was afraid. She didn't know what would happen to her so far away from home."

"Then why did she let him take me? If she knew what kind of man he was—"

"She didn't."

"What?"

"He just took you, Abel, from a neighbor's house while she was at work."

I needed a few seconds to deal with this. My mother was still hanging on to my hand and trying to wipe away her tears.

"There's still one thing I don't understand," I said when I felt calm enough to speak. "Why the fuck did he choose me instead of August?"

Sophie turned back to my mother and said a few words. There was such a long silence that I thought she wasn't going to answer. But then she slowly raised her head. She looked into my eyes and said something.

"You were more like her."

"You're telling me that he didn't want my brother?"

"No. I'm telling you that he wanted to hurt your mother. He thought you were her favorite."

I felt sick. I dropped my head and forced myself to breathe very slowly.

"You see," Sophie continued, "your mother's not only apologizing because you grew up with Louis. She can't forgive herself for not coming to find you."

My mother struggled to speak again.

"She says that she was trying to raise your brother on her own and there just wasn't any money to come to the States. She thought your father would change your names to avoid the police. And . . . she was afraid of him."

I let out a harsh breath.

"Tell her it wouldn't have fucking mattered. He wouldn't have let me leave with her. And she never would have survived living with him."

My mother began crying harder. I went down on my knees and took her into my arms. "Don't cry, Mama. Please, don't cry. It wasn't your fault. You tried to look out for me—"

Sophie stood up and quietly left the room.

I'd been sober for seven years when Serge and I had our first—and only—major fight.

It was winter, during that space when January crawls into February and it's dark in the morning and dark by dinnertime. The whole damn world gets sucked into a black hole. It's like you're spending your life in a tunnel.

It was Angie's birthday and Serge called to invite me to meet them at an Italian restaurant near their crib in Brooklyn. And he told me to bring someone.

"Damn, man—I'm really not seeing anybody right now."

"You could use this as a chance to get something going with someone. How about Grace, that girl who works at FAO Schwarz? She's single, kinda smart and looks pretty good, too—"

"I know you're not trying to hook me up with some chick from our meeting."

"Well, why the hell not? At least she'd understand how you see things."

"Being in a group don't mean shit, Serge. You know damn well that lots of people who come to meetings don't have it together at all—"

"It won't hurt you to ask her out on a date."

"If I ask one of those bitches out they'll be mailing the wedding invitations the following week. I can't be bothered with any shit like that."

"Let's get real, buddy," he said, and I heard something in his voice I'd never heard before. "What you can't be bothered with is anybody who wants some truth."

"What the fuck does that mean?"

"It means that maybe it's time for you to come clean about the way you treat the women in your life."

"There is no woman in my life."

"No, but there's about fifty women in your bed. And each one of them thinks she has a shot at being the only one—"

"I don't give them any reason to think that."

"But you don't give them any reason not to. It's fucked up, Abe. Because those women have feelings, whether you want to see it or not."

"I don't lie to any of them."

"But you don't tell them the truth, either. That's just some bullshit to pretend that silence is the same thing as honesty. And it's time for you to be honest with someone—starting with yourself."

"What the hell are you talking about?"

"It's part of what you're supposed to be doing. You know, listing the people you've harmed. And being willing to set things straight so you won't continue to act like an addict when you're trying to live clean."

"Are you telling me that seven years of sobriety don't count for shit?"

"I'm telling you that sobriety is a process. You're supposed to get stronger. Better. You're supposed to grow."

"I don't have to grow on your terms."

"You're not even growing on your own. This fuck-whoever-I-can mentality needs to end, Abe. You need to recognize that you have a responsibility to other people. And especially to those women who want to be a part of your life. You need to own your behavior, in the past, present and future."

"Who are you to say this shit to me? You know you've done your share of dirt to Angie."

"Yeah, I've screwed up more than once. And I regret it royally. But this isn't about me."

"You're trying to talk like you're my fucking father—"

"Nobody in your father's whole goddamn life ever made him accountable for what he did to you. Nobody ever asked him to be a responsible man. But I'm not gonna let you get off that damn easy, because I believe you're worth more than the life you're leading. You've got to believe that you can be a better human being. And you've got to work for it."

I knew that every single word he said was right. But I wasn't ready to hear it.

"Maybe I'm fine with the way things are," I answered. "I don't feel like wasting my time thinking about shit that went down in the past."

"This is about freeing yourself from that shit, Abe."

"I'm already free because I don't give a shit."

"You don't even see how much better your life could be."

"Maybe I don't want to end up a holier-than-thou asshole like you."

I felt a bittersweet victory when he didn't answer. There was a long silence before he said anything. When he did, his voice was low and cool.

"All right. The party's tomorrow night at eight. Hope you can make it."

———

"I wish you could do something to help your brother."

Sophie and I were waiting to catch the train back to Amsterdam. I was standing right beside her, watching her cigarette smoke disappear in the darkness and hating my father with every once of strength in my body.

"That asshole doesn't want my help."

"But he needs it."

"To tell you the truth, Sophie, I really don't give a shit."

"He's your brother, Abel."

"Maybe."

"You saw his picture."

"That picture doesn't make him my brother."

"And your anger doesn't make him a stranger."

I looked down at her. Those dark eyes stared up at me, cool and defiant. I wanted to hurt her.

"Just because you're on some fucked-up save-the-sinner trip with your junkie sister doesn't mean I have to give a shit about what happens to that crackhead."

"You should try to understand him, Abel."

"Why? He lied to me about every goddamn thing. Even his name."

"He's sick."

"Not *that* sick."

"Do you really think he chooses to live that way?"

"He could make the choice to get out. I did, Sophie. And so did you."

"You've forgotten what it means to live between shots of liquor. Or bottles of beer—or whatever shit you drank."

"I didn't hurt other people when I was drinking—"

"Don't try that crap with me. I know *exactly* what addicts do.

We spend every moment of our lives lying to someone when we're using."

"But this isn't about me!"

"Of course it is. You hate August because he's everything you fear in yourself."

"I've got a job, a crib and I don't drink anymore."

"But you're afraid, Abel. Every moment of every day you're afraid you may start drinking again. When you walked into Vetiver's that first morning, I took one look at you and I knew. It's there, in your eyes, like a dog pulling at his leash so hard he's almost choking. I thought, 'Look, Sophie. He's Black. He's in recovery. And like you, he doesn't trust anyone or anything.' "

"So the fuck what?"

"So stop hating them, Abel. Stop blaming your mother for loving your father. Stop hating your father, even though he's dead. And stop thinking that nobody in this world has ever hurt as much as you."

For a hot minute Louis rose up in me. But something inside of me said, Look, fool: You need to listen.

Sophie was still staring at me. She brought her hand up to my face.

"Try to help him, Abel. Help him the way other people have helped you."

"I can't."

"You can." Sophie paused. She started to look at me with those cold eyes again. "Let me tell you why I know that you can.

"It's my fault Saskia was strung out," she continued. "She read the letters I was sending home from Amsterdam. She believed that I was working in a big store and earning good money. She thought I had a beautiful apartment and a wonderful boyfriend. So she followed me and found me in my window."

"You didn't send her away?"

"Of course not. I showed her my money, my clothes——"

"You made her believe that you liked being a whore?"

"I didn't have to make her believe it. I loved being wanted. I loved the money and the sense of power I had over my johns. And I loved getting high. So I got her high, too, and set her up right beside me.

"Even after I got clean, it took me a long time to deal with what I'd done to my sister. I'd been out almost five years before I found the courage to try to save her. So I don't feel like I have the right to judge anyone else. Least of all someone who's still using, like your brother."

Things were fucked up between us all the way back to Amsterdam. I wanted to say something to make it right. It obviously hurt her to admit what she'd done to her sister. But I wasn't ready to say what she wanted to hear.

Things got even more fucked up the minute I stepped off the train.

"I'll walk you home, Sophie."

"I'm not going home and I don't need you walking me anywhere."

She vanished into the crowd, swallowed up in the rush of people pouring through the terminal and out into the night. Someone touched my arm and a dude in blackface, wearing a purple robe and a toy crown, shoved a fistful of candy at me.

Laughter exploded from a bunch of guys in studded leather who were passing a bottle between them. I backed into an old couple who held up their umbrellas like I was some kind of animal. I fell in step behind a group of teenagers beat-boxing a rap by Eminem. One looked in my direction and I saw a swastika tattooed above her left eyebrow.

I made my way to the street and paused near the taxi stand just outside the station. Hundreds of people were milling around me.

Suddenly I was thrust into a loneliness so deep that if I had been able to put my hands on a bottle I would have nuked my twelve years of sobriety. I closed my eyes and welcomed back my Thirst.

When I opened my eyes my vision fastened on a Heineken sign blinking across the street from the train station. Feeling as if a rope was tied around my belly, I lurched forward and started walking toward it.

I can't fucking do this, I thought. I can't throw twelve goddamn years of struggle away.

But the trembling in my hands had already moved to my lips and then down to my knees, and another voice kicked in.

Come on, Abel. After such a long time, you know you're man enough to handle one simple beer. Look at all the fucking things you got to celebrate: You've found your mother! Then you found out you've got a brother! Hell, you should even be celebrating the fact that your goddamn son of a bitch father finally did you a favor and checked out.

I didn't bother to look left or right. No motherfucking car was going to hit me now. I didn't even slow down at the door of the bar. I pushed it open and greeted the life I'd abandoned twelve years before.

Big damn surprise: Nothing had changed.

I may have gone halfway around the world, but the smells, the sounds and even the taste of the air was the same. Some kind of electronic game blinked in the corner. Female voices were mixed with hard male laughter, and some white boy was screeching out a heavy-metal tune.

I crossed the room and sat down at the bar.

"Beer."

"Light or dark?"

"Dark."

Seconds later a foam-capped glass stood before me. I slowly closed my fist around its waist. I felt the cool beads of condensation against my palm. How could anything this beautiful cause me any pain?

I raised the glass slowly, enjoying its weight. I breathed in the sweet tang of the malt. Pressed the rim against my lips, savoring the end of that terrible emptiness called Sobriety.

But then something stirred in me—something as new and yet as old as the sense of safety I'd felt when my mother held me in her arms. It may sound stupid, but for the first time in as long as I could remember, I felt like I was loved.

Slowly I lowered the glass. I pulled a handful of euros from my pocket and laid them carefully on the counter. Then I stood up shakily and walked to the door like I was wading through swiftly rising waters.

A young cat came out just as I reached the steps of the row house.

"Excuse me. I'm looking for someone called Saskia."

"Saskia? I don't know. Maybe you try the top flat."

I entered the dark hallway and began to climb. When I reached the seventh floor I knocked quietly.

"*Ja?*"

"Sophie—it's me. Abe."

The door opened a few inches. A woman called out from behind her.

"I really can't talk right now."

The woman called out again, and Sophie responded in Dutch. She looked wearily at me. "Since you're here, you might as well come in."

Saskia's crib was little more than a rough, unfinished attic. The ceiling was so steeply sloped that I could stand up straight only in the center of the room.

She didn't have much: a table, a couple of scuffed and mismatched kitchen chairs; a hot plate on a bed stand and a mattress covered with a stained comforter. A single hanging lamp with an orange shade cast a sick glow over the clothes strewn across the floor.

"My sister's having a shitty night."

From the looks of things, her whole life was shit. A toilet flushed, and Saskia came out of the back in a robe and socks.

Her head was now short, dark bristles—she'd been wearing a wig at the meeting—and her face was a younger, street-worn version of Sophie's. The bruise I had noticed earlier formed a shadow from her eye socket to her chin. She looked at me without recognition until Sophie said something in Dutch. Then she walked past us and slumped into a chair.

"Can I help?"

"No," Sophie answered, her eyes following her sister.

"How about something to eat?"

"Hashish," Saskia said loudly. "I'll start with hash."

"No, you won't," Sophie said. "But some food isn't a bad idea."

"I'm not hungry."

"The Thai restaurant on the corner should still be open," Sophie said, ignoring her. "Maybe you could get some fried rice and something with chicken. Not too spicy, though. Her stomach can't handle much."

I left and returned a few minutes later with several cartons of food. I joined Sophie at the table, where she tried to convince her sister to eat.

Saskia lifted her head and shot me a you-can-have-some look. I looked away. Then she shoved the sleeves of her robe up past her elbows. Between the tattoos, rows of fine slashes stood out pink and raw.

She began picking at a carton of fried rice, her forehead shining with sweat. Her breath was shallow and her knee bounced nervously against the leg of the table. Sophie was toying with a carton of stir-fried snow peas. Suddenly I knew that they were waiting for something.

A loud banging on the door made Sophie leap out of her chair and jog across the room before Saskia could do anything. A male voice called out in a strange mixture of Dutch and English. Sophie answered, obviously refusing to let the man come in.

They argued. Saskia sat very still, her head down. The man called out to her, and Saskia started to get up, but Sophie turned and stared her down. I stood up, too, but Sophie raised her hand.

"Saskia—Saskia! Look at me."

Saskia reluctantly obeyed.

"Do you want to go with him?"

There was a heavy pause. Then Saskia shook her head and looked away.

Sophie turned back to the door. "Go fuck yourself, Nils. She doesn't want to see you anymore."

The man shouted something back. I crossed the room and opened the door, coming face-to-face with a very blond cat at least a head shorter than me. His eyes widened as he took in my physique and height. I could smell the liquor on his breath.

"Listen, motherfucker," I said calmly. "I'll kick your punk ass if you don't get the fuck out of my sight."

The man turned and actually ran down the steps. It was almost funny.

Sophie walked back to her sister. "I thought you told him you're finished."

"I did."

"Then why did he come?"

The answer was in Dutch.

"Would you have gone with him if I wasn't here?"

"Nils loves me."

"He loves you selling yourself to pay for his shit."

"I don't care."

"You have to care."

"Fuck you." Saskia dropped her head onto her folded arms.

Sophie sat down. She picked up the carton of snow peas, stared into it, then set it down again.

Her face had the look of distant coldness I now recognized from the day we met.

Something unfolded in my mind, and I knew exactly what to do.

"Sophie," I said quietly, "did I ever tell you about LT?"

"What?"

"LT—that is, Little Tre. My best friend when I was a kid. Or I guess I should say, the only friend I ever had when I was a kid."

I could see that what-the-hell-is-he-talking-about look on her face. But I could also see that she was glad I was breaking up that cut-your-goddamn-throat silence.

So I just started talking.

"Little Tre was this tiny little guy with big damn eyes. I mean, enormous eyes. Not just puppy-dog eyes—eyes like cartoon dogs and cats that can break your heart with one damn look. And he knew how to use those eyes, too. He could get anything he wanted just by smiling at somebody and looking all pitiful.

"For example, all of us was on welfare or worse. The school had to give us breakfast and lunch, and LT figured out how to go from kid to kid and get their applesauce and chocolate milk just by sitting down and looking at them for about ten seconds. I mean he never said shit. Never bullied anybody. Never had to plead or beg. The kids would just hand the shit over and practically thank him for taking it.

"He always wore the same clothes to school—a pair of black pants with more patches than pants, and a white T-shirt with a faded-out picture of Mighty Mouse on it. And let me tell you— those might have been his only clothes, but they were always clean.

"Now we were in the first grade. Six years old or so. And LT was the smallest, and without a doubt, the smartest kid in the class. He didn't do much schoolwork—well, the teacher was having a hell of a time teaching any of us to read—but LT, unlike the rest of us, never could get into any trouble. He could play around, drop his pencil and break his crayons all day, but the teacher never seemed to get mad. The rest of us could count on getting the ruler over our knuckles if we tried any of his shit.

"One day LT said he had to go to the bathroom. Our classroom had a toilet in the corner with two or three little stalls. All the rest of us were sitting on the floor in a circle around the teacher. I think she was reading something to us.

"All of a sudden we heard this tiny little high-pitched voice coming out of the stall: '*Oh baby, baby! I want to know*—'

"The teacher stopped reading and looked over toward the toilet. '*Oh baby, baby, I need you so*'—

"Everybody turned around and just listened to Little Tre

singing his heart out: *'Oh baby, baby, please do not go! I got the Mis-sissippi lonely-man blues. . . .'*

"We started to laugh, but the teacher hushed us. I mean, she was completely blown away as LT went on singing:

Oh, baby, baby, don't go away,
Oh, baby, baby, please say you'll stay,
Oh, baby, baby, right here I pray
I got the Mississippi lonely-man blues.

"When LT came out of the bathroom the teacher said, 'Oh my Lord, child! Where did you learn to sing like that?' And LT turned those big eyes on her and said, 'My grandpappy teach me, Mrs. Knight.' And the teacher got tears in her eyes and gave us recess for the rest of the afternoon.

"From that day on LT had to sing every day. He had to sing 'America the Beautiful' before we said the Pledge. 'This Land Is Your Land' at lunch. And lead us in 'The Star-Spangled Banner' right before we went home. Sometimes she'd send him around to sing those songs in other classes, too.

"The problem was, LT didn't like singing that kind of music. He got tired of having to sing the same shit every day, too. So one day on the playground he said to me, 'Abel, I got to figure out a way to make her leave me alone.' And I said 'Why you want to do that? The teacher like you. You don't have to do all the stuff we do.' And he said, 'There ain't no point in being so different. I just like to sing, that's all.' 'Well, I got an idea,' I said. 'Maybe if you do this she'll let you quit.'

"Well, the next day Mrs. Knight sent LT up to the front of the room, as usual, to sing 'America the Beautiful.' All the rest of us kids had to stand up, face the flag and put our hands on our hearts. Then LT started to croon in his tiny voice:

Sistah Betty, bring them big-ass thighs to me,
Sistah Betty, I love those titties can't you see?
Sistah Betty won't you spend the night with me?
I want some of that sweeeet pu—

"Poor Little Tre never got to finish his song, because Mrs. Knight picked him up around the waist and literally threw him into the bathroom. We could hear him yelling and gurgling and spitting while she washed his mouth out with soap. We all wanted to laugh, but we were scared that if she heard us she'd wash our mouths out, too. So we just stood there, still holding our hands on our hearts, pretending to look at the flag and waiting for Little Tre's punishment to end.

"Well, Mrs. Knight never made Tre sing to us anymore. And Tre was happy. When I saw him on the playground the next day he said to me, 'The soap really didn't taste all that bad. I was making all that noise so she'd think she got me good. You know how it is: A man's gotta do what a man's gotta do.' "

Sophie laughed out loud and clapped her hands. Saskia raised her head and actually smiled at me. I saw something in her eyes—maybe a little bit of joy. I felt some of that joy, too.

Sophie got her into bed while I sat at the table, smoking one of my last Newports. After a while she joined me, picking up the empty food cartons with a sigh.

"She'll sleep through the night."

"You sure?"

"Yes. She's always been that way. Even when we were little. She has a hard time with the simple things—eating, getting to sleep, cleaning up—but once you get her started, she does okay."

"Who was that man who came here earlier?"

"That was her boyfriend, Nils. He's a Swedish guy who

moved here a few years ago. He got on the needle, lost his job, and ended up on the streets. Even though Saskia's clean, he's still using and he wants to put her back out there." Sophie cast a weary look toward the bed. "She's kept him high for a long time. As you can see, she did nothing for herself."

"Who pays the rent?"

"An outpatient rehab program. I buy her food, but Nils takes everything else and sells it for drugs."

"Can she get a job?"

"She doesn't have any skills. She'll need to go back to school when she's stronger."

"Can't she help out at the café?"

"Elias doesn't want her around. He says she'll steal."

"But she's your sister—"

"That doesn't mean anything to some people."

I felt a stab of shame. Sophie stood up, went over to the bed and covered Saskia with a blanket. I watched as she stood there for a few seconds, just looking at her sister.

Then she came back and picked up her bag. "We can go now. Nils won't come back if he thinks you're here."

Out on the street I took her hand and brought it to my lips.

"Come back to the hotel with me."

"I'm tired, Abel."

"Sophie, you spend your life taking care of everybody around you. Just for tonight, let me take care of you."

I like the way Sophie feels just after she comes. Soft in every part of her body. Her skin's alive, her eyes get real deep and for a few minutes she forgets about everything.

She can keep on coming if I stroke real gently just inside her thighs, or trace her nipples with just the tip of my tongue. And then, if I put my tongue on that pebble in the folds of satin skin, I can almost make her cry.

You see, Sophie likes it real slow, and as deep as I can go. She likes my weight on top of her, and she answers every thrust with a soft sound in the back of her throat. Her nipples are hard against my chest and I feel her pull me closer and wrap her thighs tighter around my back.

It's all I can do to keep from exploding, but I want her to get there before me. I want to feel the tremor inside of her. I want her to open up her eyes and know that it's me who's bringing her home.

So I'm calling her name and her thick lashes tremble and then I see it in her face and I know she sees it in mine. I give her everything I've got and her hips answer. We're pulling and pushing and then she cries out and we're somewhere else and something close to pain rockets through my body.

There are tears in her eyes. I'm thinking: I love you, woman.

I wipe her face with my fingers and hold her so tight I think it must hurt. But she's holding me even tighter.

And I say: "I love you, woman."

Then, before the feeling's gone, I roll her gently on top of me and start making love to her once again.

In the warm, dark night we talk.

"You know, here we are, doing this—" I stop stroking her breast and touch her face, "and I still don't know that much about you."

"You know more than most people."

"But I want to know more."

"Like what?"

"Like, for instance—" I kiss that luscious mouth, "what do you like to eat?"

"To *eat*? Let's see. I like Bami Goreng—"

"Now, what is that?"

"It's from Thailand. And I also like curry."

"Curry? That's what they eat in India."

"And in Suriname, where my parents were born."

"Speaking of which"—I lean over and speak real softly in her ear—"I don't even know your full name."

"Sophia Khalilah de Vries."

"Khalilah?" I kiss the soft skin along her throat. "Isn't that Arabic?"

"The Indian half—" she draws in her breath, "of my family was Muslim, but the Blacks were Cath—"

I do something with my hand that makes her stop talking.

"Sophia Khalilah de Vries is all right," I say a little bit later. "But Sophia Khalilah Crofton sounds a whole lot better."

"What are you talking about?"

"I'm talking about you and me."

"Come on, Abel. You're moving way too fast."

"All right," I answer. "The lady wants to see what we can do real slow. . . ."

After a while, I ask her what she likes to listen to.

"Youssou N'Dour."

"You *what*?"

"He's a singer from Senegal. And I really love Seal."

"Okay. But neither one of those cats can do it like us brothers from Harlem."

To prove that I spend more some time kissing her. All over.

Then I look into her eyes.

"Sophie, I want to know how you got out."

She releases a long breath. "Well, one night one of my regulars, a guy named Ian, came in. I didn't expect to see him till that weekend—he was a teacher who took the ferry over from England on the last Saturday of every month.

"Ian was a good guy. A gentleman. Paid in cash. Never drunk or mean. But that night something was wrong. I could see it. Which was strange, because I was always high when I was working.

"He said that he wouldn't be coming back anymore. He had traveled all the way from England to tell me that he'd taken a blood test and it came back seropositive for HIV. He had already started treatment, and he didn't want to risk exposing me. He said 'Sophie, you've always been so good to me. It's time you started being good to yourself.'

"After he left I couldn't get his words out of my head. You see, I had never thought about myself as a real person. I didn't have any hopes or dreams, and couldn't deal with my past or my future.

"So one day I took all my shit, threw it in a garbage can and set it on fire. I walked down the street to a rehab clinic and signed myself in. It took me a long time to start getting my life together, but I stayed."

"Then you met Elias."

"Yes. I had been clean for a year, and I moved into the halfway house."

"You fell in love with him?"

"I was thankful for the stability he offered me. But I still had a lot of work to do. I was so angry at everyone—my parents, my brothers, Klaus, and even Saskia. It took me years to understand that I had to forgive them—and myself—if I wanted to feel any peace."

"What happened with Elias?"

"As I got stronger I didn't need him as much anymore. He

started seeing other women, but it really didn't matter. By then the only thing I cared about was trying to save Saskia."

She reaches up and strokes my face. "I'm still not as strong as I'd like to be. But I'm getting there."

I catch her wrist in my hand and wait until she looks into my eyes.

"You *are* strong, woman. Don't ever doubt that."

She's trying to tell me about things I don't understand: Dedicating her life to saving her junkie sister. Letting go of the past in order to build a future. Finding strength and courage after years of weakness. Loving herself enough to really care about somebody else.

It's there, in her words, in her silences, in her touch. She wants me to go there with her.

"You think I should try to find him."

"What do you think?"

"I can't help him, Sophie."

"He can't help himself."

"I've already got a life."

"But he doesn't."

"Why should I do it?"

She's very quiet for a few minutes. "Because you love him," she says.

Sophie's lying in my arms, her small body warm and soft and brown.

"It's your turn, now," I say. "What do you want to know?"

She reaches for a cigarette and lies back in bed, kicking the sheets away from our bodies.

"Do you have a woman at home?"

"There's someone I see sometimes."

"Is she in love with you?"

"I don't know. I realize that sounds like some bullshit, but it's the truth."

"Do you live together?"

"I've never lived with anybody."

"Because?"

"For a long time it was just me and the bottle. Then after I got clean I didn't want anybody to fuck with that."

She's quiet for a while. Then her voice gets real low.

"Abel, do you hit them?"

"Who?"

"Your women."

My muscles tense but I keep my voice light. "Now what are you talking about, baby?"

"I'm talking about your father, and what he did to you."

"I'm not my father."

"But do you ever turn into your father?"

"Where is this coming from?" I lean up on one elbow and look into her face.

"Answer me."

"All that shit is over, Sophie."

Her black eyes hold mine. "Answer me, Abel."

"You don't understand. Things are different now. I've never known a woman like you."

"Do you know what I want from a man? More than anything in the world? I want honesty."

I look down at her and something moves over inside of me.

"I'll try to get there, Sophie. Just give me a little more time."

I just didn't know how to do it.

Make amends, I mean. Right the wrongs. Set things straight. Whenever I sat down and tried to think about all the people—the women, in particular—I'd hurt over the course of my life, I had to give up. There were just too damn many.

And then there was that thing with the money. It wasn't something I was very proud of, but when I was a kid I stole from Vanelle all the time. She kept her money in an envelope stuck beneath her mattress, the way Grandma had done. It didn't take me long when I was a teenager to figure out that she wasn't keeping very good track of her savings. I could go in, lift a ten-spot or a twenty, and she never seemed to miss it. Or at least she never said shit about it.

I would use that money to buy all kinds of crap: music, weed and liquor, and later on, pussy. Even when I started working, I would reward myself with a little cash from her kitty whenever I was in the mood.

And then one day all that changed. I was about seventeen, and I was skipping school. I thought Vanelle was at work, so I went into her stash to get some money to buy myself a bottle. I had planned to go down to the courts, shoot hoops for a while, then get some snatch from one of the bitches that was always hanging around.

I was just coming out of the back room when Vanelle walked through the door carrying a bag of groceries. We both stopped in the hall and looked at each other.

"Why?" she said.

"Why what?"

"Why you doing this to me?"

"I ain't doing shit to you."

"Don't lie to me, boy."

"I ain't lying."

"Then what you got in your hand?"

"I don't got nothin' in my hand."

"Looks like money to me."

"Pops gave this to me."

"Louis don't give you nothin' and we both know it, boy."

"He left it here and told me I could take it."

"You know you not tellin' the truth."

"I am, too."

"I been coming home to this house and cooking and washing for you every day since you was a little kid, and now I catch you stealing from me."

"I didn't ask you to be here."

"No. But I promised your grandmother that if anything happened to her I would move in here and try to keep you from ending up on the streets—or ending up a drunk, like your father. I been going to work every day to make sure there's always something for you on the table. I don't dog you and God knows I never raised a hand to you. And this is how you thank me."

"If you feel that way why the hell don't you go somewhere else?"

She just looked at me. Something changed in her face and I

realized that she had known all along that her money was missing. She hadn't said anything because she knew I didn't have a mother. She knew that Louis was no kind of father. She felt bad for me. Maybe she even kind of loved me.

But the thought that she could love me pissed me off almost more than I could stand. I shoved her hard and ran past her down the hallway, calling her every name I could think of.

When I got back home that night the crib was real quiet. I didn't realize until she didn't come home the following day that she was gone. She had moved into a boardinghouse for women that was only a few blocks away from her job at the pharmacy. I didn't see her again for many years, and when I did, she never mentioned the day I refused to come clean about stealing her money.

And I sure as hell didn't apologize.

It was just past daybreak when we left the hotel. I called myself walking Sophie over to Vetiver's. The truth is that I just wasn't ready to let her go.

We hadn't made it more than a few steps when she stopped. She was looking at some homeless woman who was trying to open the doors of the cars parked along the canal.

"Abel," she said quietly, "if your brother lives in Haarlem I think I know how to find him."

We looked at each other and she waited, the question in her eyes.

"Yeah, okay," I said after a pause. "I think we—I—should try to find him. Where do you want to start?"

"There's this place called the 'stable.' It's a squat just outside the warehouse district."

"A squat?"

"An empty building that homeless people move into. The police ignore it because the owner doesn't care who lives there."

"How do you know about it?"

She glanced at the homeless woman and shrugged. I asked her one more question. "Why is it called the 'stable'?"

"Because it was once used for animals."

Sophie's eyes were still fixed on the would-be thief, who was making her way down the street. Then she looked up at me. "Listen—I'll call Elias and tell him to open up the café. You might not find this place if I don't go with you."

In less than an hour we were in Haarlem. It was still so early that the streets were deserted.

Sophie set off through the heavy fog rising up from the canals. The houses seemed to appear out of the mist and the air smelled like wet moss and chimney smoke.

We crossed Haarlem's empty square. Then we passed through a neighborhood of row houses with yet more of those identical doors and windows. After crossing four or five canals we came to a group of low buildings.

"Looks like you know exactly where we're going," I said as she turned down yet another alley without even looking at a street sign.

"This is where I was studying when I met Klaus."

"You lived in Haarlem?"

She pointed up to the window on the second floor of a dingy brick house. "While I was in trade school I shared a room with a girl who grew up right there. She was my best friend until Klaus showed up. And then, when he asked me to go to Amsterdam, she told me she hated me. She said that he only wanted me because I'm Black, and some men prefer having sex with Black women. She said he'd make me into a whore. Of course I didn't believe her." Sophie laughed softly. "You can't imagine how many times over the years I wished I'd listened."

"What happened to Klaus?"

"Here in the Netherlands it's perfectly legal for a woman to work as a prostitute. But pimping is illegal. So Klaus was arrested and forced to leave the country. I imagine he's doing the same thing somewhere in Germany or eastern Europe."

We heard the stable before we could see it. Shrieking guitar music destroyed the peace of the morning as we came around the last row of warehouses.

The building was very old. Built with rough bricks, its exterior had a single door and rows of boarded up windows. There were bars on the few intact panes and the entrance was propped open with wooden crates.

Sophie paused. "Abel, I don't think it's safe to go in there."

"We don't exactly look like the law."

"We don't look homeless, either." She gestured toward my leather jacket. "We're a walking invitation to get robbed. Or worse."

"If August is in there—"

"There's a good chance he may be too high to help us. And I'm not sure he'd protect you from the others, anyway."

I stared at the door. I knew she was right.

"Just wait here for a few minutes. I'm going to have a quick look around."

She nodded. "All right. But if you find him, try to get him to come out here to talk."

I followed the rutted asphalt toward the stable. Although nobody seemed to be around, the loud guitar music continued. Stopping at the entrance, I could see that nothing was moving inside. The lights in the hall were smashed, with pieces of the broken globes still hanging from the fixtures. I could make out rows of low wooden partitions—stalls—and a passageway leading straight through to the rear of the building.

"Hey, August! You in here?"

I knew nobody could hear me over that guitar-in-heat.

"Hey—I'm looking for August!"

Something shifted and suddenly I realized why it was so dark in the building. The room was actually painted black. There were mattresses all over the cement floor and pieces of cardboard taped over the broken windows. It was like a barn, but it was filled with people instead of animals.

As my eyes got used to the darkness I began to make out arms and legs. Some were clothed. Others not. Shaved skulls wrapped in scarves for warmth were laying beside heads that were matted and filthy. Some people were coupled up in rumpled sleeping bags. Others slept alone. The air smelled of sweat, shit and vomit.

Carefully I crossed the room, looking left and right. Curling posters of rock stars were hung from the peeling walls. Cardboard food containers littered the corners, along with broken glass and used syringes. No one moved when I accidentally kicked over a beer bottle.

Just as I reached the end of the hall the music stopped. I could make out the silhouette of a tall man in the shadows.

"That you, August?" my voice echoed down the corridor.

"What you want?"

"I'm looking for someone named August."

A white cat holding a guitar came out of the shadows. He had bleached dreadlocks that moved like snakes in the dim light.

"Nobody with that name here."

"He's about my height and color. Plays the sax."

"What you want with him?"

"He got hurt and I want to see if he's okay."

"Why?"

"Because I was with him when it happened."

"Did you make it happen?"

"Would I be here if I did?"

"Maybe you want to finish the job and get out fast."

"I'd have to walk over a lot of people to do that."

"Maybe you think he got lots of enemies."

"Or maybe I care about him."

"Nobody care that much."

"Then why do you think I'm here?"

"Maybe he got somethin' you want."

"You mean drugs? I can get that shit on any street corner in Amsterdam."

"Not this shit."

"I don't want to buy any goddamn drugs."

"You want a woman?"

"You mean he—"

"He got a friend or two. You want white or Black?"

I wanted to puke, but I forced myself to stay cool.

"I don't think it's hard to get a woman in Amsterdam, either."

"You got something else going on with him?"

I stood there for a minute, looking at that piece of shit.

"No, man. Nothing at all."

I began to make my way back down the darkened corridor. Some of the sleepers were now beginning to move. As I reached the stable entrance I sensed that Whitelocks was behind me. He winced as he followed me into the light.

"If you want," he said, shielding his eyes with a dirty hand, "I'll tell him you stop by."

"That's fine," I replied, wrenching up my jacket zipper. "And tell him I won't be back. I'm fucking done with this!"

"You leaving?"

"Tell him I've seen enough of his Haarlem." I turned and started walking toward Sophie, who was standing at the top of the road.

"Wait a minute!" The white guy was motioning in wide circles with one arm. "What the hell is your name?"

"Just call me Stupid!" I shouted over my shoulder.

"No, man. Who the hell are you?"

I laughed coldly as I walked away. "Abel Paulus Crofton. Son of Louis Franklin Crofton and Maria Justina Van Gelder. Grandson of Ardelia Hope Crofton and Moses Freeman Crofton and"— I raised my voice even louder—"brother to no fucking one!"

I had just reached Sophie when I felt someone grab my arm. I spun around to find that Whitelocks had jogged up behind me.

"Your mother name is Van Gelder?"

"Why?"

"You don't have no brother?"

"I did once. But for all I know, the asshole's dead."

"What do you mean by that?"

"I met a man who said his name was Rex. His identity card said his name was Robert Anderson. I believe he's somebody else, so I don't know what the hell to call him."

"What was your brother name?"

"August. Why? Is that *your* name, too?"

The other man shook his head. "Don't know nobody with that name."

"Well, that's what I've been saying all my life," I said, looking back at Sophie. "My mother must have been crazy to give her kids names like Abel Paulus and August Sebastian!"

"Sebastian?" the white guy asked, his eyes narrowing. "You talking about Sebastian?"

Both Sophie and I looked up. "You know him?" she asked.

"Everybody know Sebastian. Sometime he call himself Sebee."

"I'm talking about the guy who plays the saxophone," I said.

"Yeah. He play music. He do other things, too."

"Shit! You knew who I was talking about!"

"Look, man. It's not my business to say nothing to a stranger. You show up here and ask for August, but you don't know his name Sebee."

"Is he fucking here?" I shouted.

The man's eyes darted suspiciously between Sophie and me. "I don't know. What you want with him?"

"He's my *brother*, goddammit!"

"You just say you don't have a brother!"

Sophie interrupted, speaking Dutch in a low voice. White-locks slowly relaxed. Finally he looked at me.

"You want to see Sebee. But he don't want to see nobody. He come home yesterday morning and tell me not to let nobody in."

"I need to see him," I insisted.

Still the other man hesitated. I dug in my pocket and produced a 100-euro note. He inspected it before hiding it quickly inside his shirt. He gestured for the two of us to follow him.

He led us around the outside of the stable to an outbuilding at the far end of a gravel drive. There was no sign of life, yet he stopped and banged hard with his fist before pulling the rusting door open.

The smell alone would have been enough to turn most people away, but Sophie and I stepped inside. In a far corner, wrapped in a filthy sleeping bag, was a body.

Sophie walked over and pulled a tarp away from the broken

window. Everything was flooded with cold light. There was nothing else in the room besides a waterlogged crate, topped with a few personal items—a silver lighter, a heavy gold ring and a roach clip. Beside the sleeping bag was an overturned bottle of vodka.

Sophie came and stood behind me, looking down at the man sprawled on the icy floor. I crouched down and touched his throat.

"Is he breathing?"

"Barely." I looked over at the white boy. "Why is everything so damned quiet? Is everybody stoned out of their minds?"

He shrugged. "I come back late and find all of them like this. Maybe they try some new shit."

Sophie knelt beside me and touched August. "He's too cold, Abel."

I pulled the sleeping bag away and let out a breath when I saw an elastic band still tied around his upper arm. The sleeve was rolled up past the elbow. We could see that his arm was blue.

She took out her phone.

"No *politie,*" Whitelocks said.

She answered him in Dutch. He responded and they argued until I called her sharply.

"Look at this."

I peeled back the filthy shirt. The red flesh around the knife wound was swollen with pus-filled blisters. It stank like hell.

The white boy backed away, then broke into a run, his footsteps grinding up the gravel path toward the road. Sophie completed the call and turned to me.

"The ambulance will be here in a few minutes. I'll go up to the street to wait. Will you be all right?"

"He can't do shit to me."

She walked out quickly. I heard her steps fade into silence.

I reached over and picked the ring up from the crate. Carefully I made my way to the window and held it up to the light.

The inside of the band was etched with the words LOUIS FRANKLIN CROFTON 1952.

A bitter chuckle rolled up from deep inside my chest.

Louis would have loved this, I thought. After almost forty-three years of having no idea I even have a brother, I arrive just in time to watch him die.

Something stirred in the pile of rags and I saw August lift his hand and bring it to his chest. His eyes opened and fastened blankly on me. His cracked lips moved, but nothing came out.

I went back and squatted down beside him. I took his fingers in mine.

"Listen to me, you fool," I said. "It's too late for you to pretend you don't have a brother. I went to a lot of goddamn trouble to find your shitty ass, and you better not leave me now."

His fingers tightened on my hand. He was hanging on to life—but I don't know whether it was his or mine.

Late afternoon. And we were still waiting for the doctors to figure out whether he was going to make it.

Sophie was standing beside me, staring out the window at a courtyard of naked trees and rosebush stumps. She wasn't saying much, but her being there seemed to hold me together. Or maybe I was coming apart.

"I lied to you."

I'd been thinking the words as I looked at her. Thinking them, but sure as hell not planning to say them.

She didn't move. Didn't even turn her head. It was like she'd been waiting for this to happen.

"You—well, you asked me last night if I ever turned into Louis when I was drinking. And the answer is yes. I did then, and sometimes I still do now. The fucked up thing is—I never thought it was wrong."

I watched her shoulders shift a little, like she was steadying herself to take on some extra weight.

"And you know that story I told you about hitting my bottom? About waking up in that girl's room and puking all over myself in the street? Well, most of that was bullshit, too."

She still didn't react. And all of a sudden I couldn't have stopped myself, even if I had wanted to.

"The truth is that I woke up in that girl's bed. I started hitting her when she asked for her money. I was slapping her around when her little girl came into the room. And I was still beating her when her pimp got to the door. That's the reason I had to use the fire escape to get out."

My body started to shake. I waited, wondering if I'd have the guts to tell her everything. She waited, too, without making a sound.

"She was just a kid, Sophie. Just a kid. But I was willing to fuck her and then beat her. To be honest, it was only right that her pimp caught up with me and kicked my alcoholic ass, right there on the sidewalk. Because that was the end. That's when I knew I was going to die. My soul was already dead.

"But there's other shit, too. I've hurt a lot of women and enjoyed it. I've fucked other men's wives, then smiled in their faces. I stole money from someone who cared about me. And I have never in my life apologized to anyone for anything."

I felt her reach up and take my hand. And my next words just spilled out from someplace so deep that I had never even come close to going there before.

"I did that shit, and a lot of other shit, because I have always felt so goddamn powerless. Even now, at this very minute, I don't know any other kind of man to be."

Sophie finally looked up at me. Her eyes searched mine. Then, smiling faintly, she stood on her toes and gently kissed me.

"You're already finding him."

Her words opened something up in me. And I felt a kind of lightness—like somebody had broken through a thick stone wall and let a whole lot of clean, fresh air inside.

I had never felt anything like that before. It took me a few seconds to realize that someone was calling my name. One of the doctors had come up and was standing just a few feet away.

"Mr. Crofton? Excuse me, but may I have a word with you?"

"Hey, baby—" I turned back to Sophie, "it's getting close to your meeting." I wiped something out of my eyes. "I'll call you when I get back to the hotel."

The doctor led me into intensive care, where my brother lay covered in bandages, with a tube down his throat and a bunch of wires attached to a wall of machines.

The doctor looked at the lab results. "You are the patient's relative, I presume?"

"I'm his brother," I said.

"I must tell you that Mr. Van Gelder is very ill. Fortunately, when he was stabbed the knife did not injure any vital organs. A person in normal health would have recovered in a few days. But Mr. Van Gelder's addiction to heroin has caused his immune system to crash. And the fact that he is seropositive for HIV only complicates the situation."

I guess a part of me knew all along. But hearing those words from the doctor's mouth seemed to change everything.

"Was he trying to kill himself?"

"I doubt it. We have thirteen other patients from that warehouse. I would guess that their supplier gave them all a poisonous substance. We'll know more when our tests are completed."

I drew in a long breath. "Is there something I can do? I mean, does he need a transfusion or anything?"

The doctor placed his hand on my shoulder. "Not at this time. But your brother is very lucky that you went to look for him. Without your help he would already be dead."

"Is he going to make it?"

"We don't know yet. He is heavily sedated and probably won't be able to speak until tomorrow morning. If you'd like, you can stay with him for a while."

I looked over at the wall of monitors. Suddenly I was afraid that he would die the way Louis had died, leaving me with nothing but his hate.

I knew I wasn't ready to deal with that shit.

At least, not that day.

I arrived at the residence just as the old folks were filing down the halls to the dining room for supper. Lots of the men were wearing suits and ties and the women had on dresses and jewelry.

"Mr. Crofton!"

The director, Marta Blankenvoort, walked toward me with a smile. "I'm glad to see you this evening. Might we speak for a moment?"

I sat down as Marta settled into the leather chair behind her desk.

"The supervisor has reported to me that Mrs. Van Gelder has made remarkable progress since you started coming to see her a few days ago. Our speech therapist has been working with her for months, but now, for the first time, she is really trying to overcome her paralysis."

"Yes, I noticed that she even seemed to understand some English."

"Understand some English? Then you didn't know that Mrs. Van Gelder was an English teacher? Mr. Crofton, in cases of paralysis many patients find it very difficult to speak their own language. It is even harder to speak a foreign language. I promise you that Mrs. Van Gelder has understood everything you said to her, even if she was unable to reply. For over thirty years she

worked in the secondary schools, training students who wished
to work in the public sector. She has many former students who
really love her." Marta smiled. "I suppose you can tell that I'm
one of them."

"I—I didn't know. There's so much I don't know. Maybe you
can help me with something. Did Mrs. Van Gelder ever talk
about her son?"

"You are asking about August Sebastian."

"You know him?"

"We went to school together. He was always . . . a very angry
boy. He had many fights. He missed many classes. The teachers
didn't know what to do with him."

"But—but was he close to my—I mean, to Mrs. Van
Gelder?"

"She tried very hard with him. But she was divorced, and being a single mother was more difficult in those days."

"She never married again?"

"No, although I'm sure she could have. She was a very pretty
woman, and very talented."

"What about the rest of her family?"

"She explained to me once that she had lost her parents just
after the war, when she was quite young. That's what brought
her to Amsterdam. She learned to speak English from her husband, who was an American soldier. Later she returned to college and prepared herself to teach."

"I guess—well, it's pretty obvious that I'm also her son. August Sebastian is my brother. My father took me away to the
States when I was just a baby and I never made it back."

"I saw the resemblance the first time you came," Marta said.
"But—actually I thought it would be impolite to inquire. I suppose that Mrs. Van Gelder didn't know where you were living?"

"That's right."

"Well, the important thing is that you're here now."

When I didn't answer the director reached across her desk to touch my arm.

"Your mother's condition was very serious when she moved into this residence. The doctors didn't know if she would ever walk or speak again. Her depression was so deep that we feared she might try to take her own life. As a teacher, your mother found great power in her ability to communicate. The loss of that power was almost more than she could bear.

"I believe Mrs. Van Gelder found a new reason to live from the day of your first visit. She has requested physical therapy to improve her walking. She is eating better and taking an interest in her appearance. I am sure that this is all due to you."

"No, I don't think that's possible."

"Mr. Crofton, how much longer will you be in the Netherlands?"

"Just a few more days."

"Is there any way that you could extend your visit?"

"I've got to be back at work next week."

"Perhaps you could return in the near future?"

"I don't really know."

"Then, I take it that you don't know how your mother became ill."

"No."

"Well, it is not my province to reveal this, but I think that you should know. One night August Sebastian came into her house and tried to rob her. He was high on drugs, and when she refused to give him money he became very angry. They argued and your mother collapsed. He took whatever he could find and left her there. Your mother is alive today because her neighbor saw the lights on and the open door in the middle of the night."

"You're sure about this?"

The director nodded. "She had supported August Sebastian for many years. It seems that when she finally retired from teaching he became more and more angry that she couldn't continue to give him money."

"Did the police catch him?"

"Your mother refused to press charges. But it made no difference—he had already vanished. Certainly he's changed his name. And, considering that he was very sick with his addiction, he may no longer be living."

"Then my mother hasn't seen him since—"

"No. When the hospital was ready to release her, I arranged for her to come and live here. She allowed me to put her house in Haarlem under the management of an agency, and they have rented the downstairs apartment. Her doctors thought that she might one day be strong enough to go home, but frankly, she wasn't making the progress we'd hoped for. That is, until you arrived."

Marta walked me through the empty dayroom. I could hear "Silent Night," sung in Dutch, coming from the dining room.

"Do the residents sing like this every evening?"

"When you travel," she responded kindly, "it is often easy to lose track of time. Today is Christmas Eve, Mr. Crofton. And . . . if I am not mistaken, this is also your mother's birthday."

The door to my mother's apartment was open and I heard the television from inside. I paused at the threshold, kind of ashamed of the flowering cactus and Belgian chocolates I'd run across the street to buy.

I should have come up with something better than this shit, I thought. I adjusted my collar and smoothed down my hair. Looking myself over quickly, I realized my shoes were still muddy from the stable.

"Oh, Abel Paulus!"

"How're you doing?" I asked, walking forward and kneeling down to give her an awkward hug.

I sat across from my mother, then realized that I was still holding the candy and the cactus. I offered them to her like a schoolboy.

"Happy Birthday . . . Mama."

She laughed and held out her arms for another hug. I helped her open the chocolates, and she selected one and bit into it with a sigh. Then she grasped my hand with easy affection.

Her color seemed better than before. She'd had her hair trimmed. Even her eyes were bright.

"When I talk slow, like this, do you understand me?"

She squeezed my fingers with her good hand.

"The lady downstairs just told me that you were an English teacher."

My mother nodded.

"I don't know what I expected, I mean, I never really gave any thought to how you lived or anything—"

I broke off at the confused expression on her face.

"Shit—I guess what I'm trying to tell you is that I was never very good in school. I mean, I dropped out when I was a kid and only went back a few years ago. I did manage to graduate from a two-year college, but it never even came into my head that you might be a teacher or something."

I was running off at the mouth and I knew it.

"What I mean to say is that I'm proud my mother was a teacher."

Something came into her eyes and for a moment the room

was very quiet. I suddenly realized that I didn't have to rush. Nobody was coming to take her away. And hell—she really wanted to hear what I had to say.

"You know, I never told anybody, but I always wanted to be an engineer. When I was in second grade this guy came to school and showed us this experiment with a circuit board. I thought it was the most incredible thing in the world that so much power could pass through those tiny colored wires. I guess it sounds stupid, but I wanted to find a way to use that power. I wanted to fix the things that wouldn't work in our building— you know, put some cheap light in those stairwells, bring some fresh air to the basement apartments and some heat to the rooms upstairs where the old folks lived.

"I used to dig around in the alley and collect old wires and pieces of glass and pretend to be fixing things. Grandma used to call them my inventions. She even got me a little tool kit once for Christmas."

I looked at my hands. "But then my grandma died and there was nobody who really cared too much about my schooling after that. Louis's sister Vanelle lived with us, but she was scared of him and didn't know what to do with me. So I just tried to stay out of their way and keep my nose on my face when Pop drank too much and came after me with his belt."

My mother squeezed my hand again and I looked up. "I'm not telling you this to upset you. I just want you to know how I ended up pulling cables through the tunnels under the city, instead of getting an office job in one of those skyscrapers."

She raised her good hand and stroked the side of my face.

I cleared my throat. "I guess it's all the same now. And I'm not complaining. I've got a job, a couple of rooms and enough cash to keep me alive."

Her brows came together and she shifted in the chair, causing the box of chocolates to slide forward on her lap. I caught it before it could fall and placed it carefully on one of the tables beside the sofa.

"Thank you, Abel," she said softly.

"You know, you would have liked my grandma Ardelia. She was a strong lady. She'd been through a lot. And then, she still had Louis to deal with. You know the hardest thing? I was always afraid I'd end up just like him. A mean, hateful drunk who didn't give a damn about anybody. Not even himself.

"But it seemed like the harder I tried to be free of him, well—the more I ended up being just like him. Here I am, forty-five years old, and I never managed to come close to really loving anyone. I live alone and only have one friend. Serge. And to be honest, he's my sponsor."

I looked into my mother's eyes. "You need to know that I'm a drunk, too. Just like my daddy. I drank from the time I was thirteen until about twelve years ago. Twenty years on the bottle and twelve spent in Thirst."

I shook my head slowly. "Sometimes it's damn hard, but I haven't given in yet."

"Son," she said very slowly, "I am very proud of *you*."

I blinked back tears and looked away. She squeezed my hand again, then pointed to one of the photographs on the crowded sideboard. I retrieved the photo and she took it from me and held it on her lap.

"My papa."

"Your father?" I looked at the tall, brown-haired man in a military uniform.

"Abel," she said, still pointing at the photo. "Abel Simon Van Gelder."

"I'm named after him?"

She nodded.

"Then that's why you gave me this name?"

"Abel is a good name. Strong name," she answered slowly.

I drew in a long breath.

"Mama, I have to tell you something, but I don't want to upset you."

She waited, her eyes fixed on my face.

"I found August."

She leaned forward in her chair and carefully formed her next words. "At the house?"

"No, he was staying—well, somewhere else. He's sick. He's in the hospital in Haarlem."

She dropped her eyes for a moment, and then looked up at me.

"Why?"

"He had an injury that got infected. The doctors don't know if . . ." Now I stopped speaking. She lowered her head and remained unmoving, her hand growing lank around my fingers.

"Are you all right?" I asked, and she raised her eyes at the concern in my voice.

"August is dying," she whispered.

"They're doing what they can for him, but—"

"I must see him," she said in a low voice. I moved closer to her and she repeated the words.

"Do you think your doctors will approve?"

"He is my son," she answered slowly, with dignity. "I will go with you."

W hen the train arrived at Amsterdam's Central Station that night I was too damned tired to care how empty it was. I exited the platform with a few stragglers and crossed the six-lane boulevard facing the terminal, hardly noticing that it, too, was nearly deserted. Something cold touched my face. Snow.

I took a shortcut through the red-light district, along a canal that led to the opera house, just across the water from my hotel. I was getting comfortable with Amsterdam's messed-up streets—so much so that I wasn't paying attention to much of anything. Not even the ho's sitting in the windows. Yes, those poor bitches were there all right—even on Christmas Eve.

And then I heard the voice.

"She sent you here for me?"

No shit. It was Saskia, painted and blond and standing in a doorway.

I stopped dead in the middle of the street. All right, I thought. She's a grown woman and she's out here because she wants to be. This isn't my damn business and I shouldn't get involved.

But hell, I said to myself. I'm already involved and this is not where she needs to be.

"Is Sophie looking for you?"

She shrugged. But there was something in her face.

"Why don't you come with me?" I said. "We'll go and find Sophie together."

"Fuck Sophie."

I was sorry, but not real surprised, to hear those words.

"Well, even if you don't want to see your sister, why don't you just walk a little while with me? I'm sure it'll be warmer if you keep moving. And maybe you can help me find my god-damn hotel."

"I'm waiting for somebody."

"I'll bet he'll stick around till you get back."

I stood there. She came out of the shadows real slow. She was holding a cigarette, and it shook when she brought it to her lips. I took a quick look at her face. She didn't seem to be high.

"Let's go," I said, like we were taking a stroll in the park. I even held out my arm, and she took it.

It was fucking cold, but the streets were bright with Christmas lights. We made it one or two blocks without speaking. Then I heard her rough voice.

"Sophie said you've been clean for a long time."

"Twelve years."

"For me, nine months."

I swallowed. What the hell would Serge say?

"That's great, Saskia." I paused. Retooled. "It gets kind of tough sometimes, you know?"

She made a low noise.

"I—I know it's real hard at first, but it will get better."

"Not better," she answered. "Only different."

She was right. There was no point in denying it.

"I miss it," she whispered. "I miss it so much."

"Sometimes I do, too."

"It's better than food. Better than sex. Better than everything."

"I hear you."

"I can't—I can't—"

"Yes you can, Saskia."

We walked a little farther, and then she stopped and looked
up at me.

"I ask Sophie and the others and there's something they won't
tell me. How do you become friends with the big empty place—
the place where it used to be?"

"I don't know what they've told you, but I'll tell you what I
know to be true: That empty place will never be your friend.
It'll always make you different from other people. It will choose
the folks you feel safe with. The few you can trust. Even the ones
you can . . ." I stumbled over the word, "love."

She drew on her cigarette as she thought about my words.

"You know, Sophie wanted me to get out with her seven years
ago. I said I want to stay with Nils. But the real reason I didn't
go with Sophie is because I was afraid. I didn't think I was
strong enough to stay clean. And I was afraid that no other man
would want me."

"Do you still love him?"

"I don't know. Everything's different now."

"He wants you to come back?"

"Yes. And some nights I hurt. I want someone to hold me.
Sophie thinks it's the drugs I want. But it's Nils. I don't know if
I can live without him."

"You can do it, Saskia. Just take it one day at a time. Or
maybe one hour. Or maybe—maybe just concentrate on getting
through this conversation."

She smiled. But her eyes were empty. Snowflakes were set-
tling on her blond wig and her thin jacket.

"Saskia, why are you out here tonight?"

"Because she left him. She left him and now she has no place to go."

"Who? Sophie?"

"I don't want to be like my sister and marry someone just so I'll have a place to stay—"

"You're saying that Sophie's left Elias?"

"She hated him but lived with him just so she could take care of me—"

"Listen, Saskia—"

Her voice was rising and she took a step away from me. "I don't want to go back to school so I can spend my life standing behind a counter or selling shoes or cleaning somebody's house. I don't want to go to meetings every day and pray for help from somebody who isn't even there."

"Hold on, now—"

"I don't want to be clean anymore!" she shouted. "Fuck you and fuck my sister! Why don't you just leave me the hell alone?"

She began to cry. We stood there in the middle of the street, the Christmas decorations swaying in the wind. And then I pulled her into my arms and held her for a long time.

The first thing I saw when we got back to Saskia's crib was Sophie's bags standing just inside the door.

So it was true.

Sophie ran up the stairs right behind us. She'd been searching the streets for her sister, and I actually saw tears in her eyes when she saw that Saskia was okay.

Soon she was moving around the attic, picking up clothes and speaking calmly in Dutch to her sister.

I couldn't stop looking at her. Where the hell did she find the guts—and the strength—to do what I was afraid to do?

Saskia finally got into bed. Sophie came over to sit with me at the table.

"She told you, didn't she?" She nodded toward her bags.

"Did this go down because of the shit I said about him?"

"No."

"Did he try to fuck with you?"

"He wasn't even there."

"Then why did you do it?"

She shook her head. "I came home from Haarlem and walked into the house. And I just stood in the front room, thinking.

"That apartment is full of things from his family and his travels. But there was nothing in that place that belonged to me. After six long years I was only the clothes in the closet. An exotic attraction that brought men into the café. Something he could say he fixed. I've known for a long time that I needed to get out. So today I packed up my things and left."

"Are you okay?"

"You're asking me if I want to use."

"Do you?"

"Of course I do." She glanced over at Saskia. "But I'm not going to."

She sighed. "I should have thought about what this would do to my sister. She was proud that I married Elias—it seemed like proof that getting clean could lead to a better life. Now that I'm on my own again she doesn't see much point in trying."

"So"—I found it kind of hard to look at her—"what happens now?"

She lit a cigarette and sighed.

"I'm going to sell my father's house and use the money to

start over. I wasn't ready to do that seven years ago, but I'm strong enough now. It'll be cheaper to live in Groningen or Utrecht. I'll find us an apartment and look for another program for Saskia."

"And what about you, Sophie?"

"I can always work in a store or a restaurant. I know how to take care of myself."

"What if somebody came along who wanted to take care of you?"

"I'm not alone, Abel."

"I know that."

"This isn't a game. It's about my sister's life."

"I know that, too."

"You'll only be here for a few more days."

There was nothing I could say to that.

I stood up. "You need anything?"

She shook her head.

"Then I'll come by in the morning."

I spent most of that night walking through Amsterdam.

Now, I fucking hate cold weather, and my hotel room would have been plenty warm. But something told me I needed to be outside. I needed to walk down streets that twisted and turned like the thoughts going through my mind.

All the pieces were laid out right in front of me. All I needed to do was put them together. But how was I going to do it, when I'd avoided it for so very long?

Sophie's words came into my head: "You should do it because you love him."

I knew she was right—I had started caring about that motherfucker the minute he stepped onto the stage, his clothes in rags, his face hidden, that sax his only means of expressing his rage.

That's why I took him in when that asshole tried to kill him. Why I kept on asking for his truth, when all he would give me was lies. And that's why I went looking for him, though he'd made it clear he didn't want to be found.

It was way too late to pretend that I could walk away, even if I had wanted to. August wasn't just my brother: he was me at another time in my life.

And then there was Marta Blankenvoort, asking in her polite way why the hell I wouldn't stay in the Netherlands. I had all the excuses on the tip of my tongue—the tunnels, my apartment, my great big New York life. But I knew that none of that shit mattered as much as my mother.

She had a house in Haarlem where I could live. I'd find some kind of job. And I would learn some Dutch—after all, my mother was a language teacher. If we gave it some time, she might recover her ability to speak. Maybe I could help her have a new life.

And finally, there was Sophie.

I had never felt the things she made me feel. No woman had even come close to opening that door and asking me to step inside. She said she wanted honesty, and I was just discovering what that meant. What would happen between us if I had the guts to go the distance?

The dawn found me standing at the window in my room, staring out at the rooftops in the growing light. A light wind carried a few drifting snowflakes toward the smoking chimneys and dark windowsills. The whole world seemed to have found some peace.

I knew I had a call to make. I crossed the room and sat on the bed, lifted the receiver and waited until the switchboard answered.

A shrill ring followed a series of clicks. A hand fumbled with the receiver. A voice mumbled something.

"Yeah?"

"Merry Christmas, buddy."

"What the fu—?" Serge dragged himself into consciousness. "Abe, do you know what time it is?"

"Seven-thirty in the morning."

"The fuck it is! It's one-thirty in the fucking night!"

"Not in my time zone."

"Oh, shit—you calling from Amsterdam?"

"I sure as hell am."

I heard him shift in bed, reach over and turn on a light. He murmured something to Angie, who said "Hey, Abe," sleepily.

"So," Serge laughed, "it's about fucking time I heard from you!"

"I've been busy."

"Not that busy."

"Exactly that busy. Listen, man, I found her."

"Your mother?"

"My mother."

"And she's glad to see you?"

"Like water in a desert."

"And you're feeling all right about it?"

"It hasn't been easy, but—Jesus, man, I did it." I paused. "Serge, I found someone else, too."

"Like a female someone?"

"Most definitely."

"Beautiful?"

"Yeah."

"And smart?"

"Beyond belief."

"Dutch?"

"Yep. But she's Black, man. Can you get to that?"

"She speaks English?"

"Better than you folks from Brooklyn."

"Single?"

"Maybe soon."

"What does that mean?"

"It's in the works."

"Did you bring this thing down?"

"God, I hope so."

"Are you sure about this?"

"This one's different, Serge. She already rewrote every rule in my book."

"Well, what's her name?"

"Sophia Khalilah."

"Ah, wisdom and knowledge."

"She's got plenty of both."

"How long she been clean?"

"How did you know—"

"You wouldn't fall for anybody who couldn't go there with you."

"What about my five years with Nee Cee?"

"You know you never gave a shit about Nee Cee."

"That's true. Sophie's been down for seven."

Serge laughed softly. "Not bad, Abe. You went over there and managed to find yourself a sister from Holland who's using the tools."

"And she's way ahead of me."

"How far?"

"You know damn well I stalled somewhere at the beginning. But this woman has made it all the way, my friend."

"Well, God knows you're in line for a little happiness."

"Not so fast, man. After I found my mother, I discovered something else. Serge, I have a brother."

"Your mother got remarried?"

"No. I have a twin brother and my father never told me."

"Good Lord!"

"Listen, he's using."

"Alcohol?"

"Smack."

The phone went silent for a few seconds. "So, what are you going to do?"

"I'm going to help him, Serge. I'm going to try to get him clean."

"That's good, man. I know you're ready to take this on."

"You showed me the way. It's my turn to follow. In fact, that's really what I called to say."

"What?"

"I called to thank you, brother."

"Don't start that shit, Abe!"

"And I want to tell you I love you."

"Knock it off!"

"I mean it. I wouldn't be here—hell, I might not be alive if it wasn't for you. And now I think I'm ready to give something back."

"I'm proud of you, Abe. And by the way, buddy—I love you, too."

A lot of folks came to Louis's memorial. I had it at the club where he played the most often, a run-down place called Xcaliber's on 137th at Broadway. The place was packed with people who'd heard my father perform over the years, women he'd been with off and on and even a couple of neighbors from back in the day.

I sat at a front table with Vanelle, listening as one by one people went up to the small bandstand and told stories about him. With Coltrane playing in the background, I heard about how funny my father could be. How damned talented he really was. And how stupid it was to challenge him to a game of poker.

Then a stranger got up—a woman with white hair, wearing a neatly pressed dress and rimless glasses. She looked like a retired civil servant.

"All of you knew Louis after he came back from the army," she told the room, which got real quiet.

"But I knew Louis from the time when he was just a boy. He used to sit on the steps and watch us girls playing hopscotch. When the other boys weren't looking, he'd even come down sometimes and give it a try.

"Louis really was a very sensitive young man. He loved nothing more than playing his saxophone. And although I'm sure that most of you don't know this, he loved classical music as much as he loved jazz. We used to listen to the Metropolitan Opera on the radio together. But we both knew back in those days that it was ridiculous for a Black man to even think about performing in a symphony. That's why he signed up for the army. His mama wanted him to do something good with his life. She didn't want him ending up in juke joints and bars."

Vanelle nodded. I was in shock. The woman continued.

"Now I won't lie—I liked Louis as much more than a friend, and I hoped that when he got back from overseas we might just settle down and make a life together. But as you all know, that was never to be. When Louis came back from over there he wasn't the same man. I never knew what happened to him. And though I often saw him on the street, he didn't have much of a mind to tell me anything about it, either.

"I understand from what you all are saying that he lived a certain kind of life. I suppose it's a life that some would choose, though I would have wished something different for him if it had been left up to me.

"So I'm here today to remember the Lou Crofton I cared for long ago. The man I always hoped would find his way back home."

His way back home.

Louis had never managed it.

But I was determined to get there.

My mother was real quiet when Sophie, Saskia, and I picked her up later that morning. I helped her into the car and got her wheelchair into the trunk. We made the short drive from Zand-voort to Haarlem without talking at all.

The same doctor was there who'd been on duty the day before. He greeted me and introduced himself to my mother.

"Mr. Van Gelder is heavily sedated, but he seems to be communicating fairly well this morning. He is extremely weak, however, so I can allow you only a very short visit."

"Saskia and I will wait outside," Sophie said as I wheeled my mother into my brother's room.

August Sebastian looked like a skeleton. His right hand was tethered to the bed frame, with an IV inserted at the wrist, and the left arm was folded and bound over his chest. His skull was hidden beneath a thin-skinned white cap—they had shaved his head—and his face was sunken and yellow in the low light.

But his eyes were open. He was looking at me.

I thought that I had never in my forty-five years on earth, seen anything like the emptiness in those eyes.

"You found me," he rasped. There wasn't much voice left.

"You made it pretty damn hard," I said.

I glanced at our mother. She was staring at him, too—but there was something else on her face.

"August Sebastian," she said, forming each syllable like her lips were made of clay.

Very slowly he let his eyes move to her face. I thought for a second that he would speak. But instead he waited—and so did I.

Justina shifted her weight. Her right hand lay limp on her knee. Her mouth was still pulled into that strange, crooked smile. Holding a tissue to her lips to wipe away the saliva, she pushed out five words:

"I love you, my son."

And there it was: *the willingness to forgive.*

The moment I heard my mother comforting the child who had put her in that wheelchair, I knew that I no longer had to hate Louis.

Because Louis had lost.

We had found each other.

It finally came home to me that I really was connected to something—no, to *someone*. And in that connection was the possibility to forgive all the people who had hurt me.

And to forgive myself.

August Sebastian was still staring at our mother. I could see a whole lot of shit in his face: Anger and disbelief. Fear and pain.

He started coughing and his whole body shook. When the coughing stopped there were tears in his eyes.

Without thinking I reached over and covered his hand with mine.

"Listen, brother, I need to tell you something. No matter what you may think, it's not over. We can make some kind of future together, if you'll let me help you."

There was a long, tense silence before he managed to speak.

"Why?"

"Because that's what I'm here to do."

"What about Harlem?"

"She'll be there when we're ready."

Something changed in his eyes. I don't know—it certainly wasn't trust. But maybe it was the beginning of a willingness to trust.

My mother wasn't trying to hide her sadness, but her gaze was clear and strong. She reached up and touched my brother's cheek. After a few seconds, tears spilling down his face, he finally turned his head away.

I pushed the wheelchair out into the hall.

"Abel."

I bent down to hear her better. She took my hand, her strength passing from her fingers to mine.

"I love you, too."

They say the first thing you learn in a foreign language is how to cuss. That really wasn't true for me. I started off with the prayer, then the steps and then a book of meditations on sobriety—just like I had when I began my life again back in the New York days.

It's funny how fast it made sense this time. I had to adjust to living in the daylight, but I caught on soon enough. And I got used to eating Bami Goreng and chicken curry—and even learned to like those French cigarettes.

The hardest thing was figuring out how to be part of a family: accepting the routines, being there for somebody else all the time. But all that came with a big paycheck: I got to see Saskia get off the streets for good. I was there when my mother graduated from a walker to a cane, and now we walk on Sundays along the beach in Zandvoort.

Sophie and I are making it together, though it isn't always so easy. She's tough. She doesn't like giving in. And she's still so much stronger than me.

But that's all right, too. Because she shows me every day what it means to love somebody. And I try to give it back in all kinds of ways.

Serge came over for a visit last summer. We were crossing the bridge over the canal near the house in Haarlem when he said it.

"You've done real good, man. You've got a home, a family and a very together woman. Now—when are you gonna start writing that book?"

"It's still too early in my brother's recovery, Serge. Right now I'm only focused on seeing him through."

Serge grinned at me and I realized what he already knew: that after so many years, I was finally winning the struggle. I had come far enough to give back to someone who needed me. That was my true recovery.

Sometimes it hurts to think about where I came from. But now I know it's the only way to understand how far I've come. I've still got some distance to travel, but at least I know that my Higher Power is the people I love, and the people who love me.

Reading Group Companion

Haarlem examines a man's redemption through his exploration of a new terrain and his discovery of new family members as he grapples with the nightmares of his past. The questions that follow are meant to enhance your discussion of the novel and spark conversation about Abel's road to recovery.

1) What are the events in Abel's life that have most influenced his ability to love another person?

2) What factors contributed to Abel's decision to return to the Netherlands and try to find his mother?

3) How has Abel's struggle with alcoholism affected his ability to interact with others?

4) Abel tells Serge that he doesn't believe in "that invisible white man in the sky." What are some of the other ways that Serge suggests that Abel might think of his Higher Power?

5) Upon arriving in Amsterdam, Abel is impressed by the clean, crime-free appearance of the city. How does this impression change over time?

6) How did Sophie come to live in Amsterdam, and how does her past continue to influence her life?

7) How is Abel's relationship with Sophie different from his relationships with other women?

8) How does Abel change when he finds his mother?

9) How does learning about August Sebastian affect Abel? How do Abel's feelings about his brother develop over the course of the novel?

10) What does Sophie teach Abel? Does Sophie learn anything from him?

11) The city of Amsterdam seems very different in many ways from New York. What new perspectives does Abel gain about his life as he spends time in Amsterdam?

12) How are issues of race and ethnicity depicted in *Haarlem*? How is Sophie's understanding of herself as a Black woman different from that of African-Americans?

13) What do we learn of August Sebastian's past? How does that information influence your perception of him?

14) Which Bible stories are referenced in *Haarlem*?

15) According to the novel, what are some of the differences in the ways that drugs and alcohol are consumed in the United States and the Netherlands? What are the differences in the ways the two nations respond to problems of addiction?

16) How does Abel's recovery from alcoholism grow through his relationships with his mother? Sophie? Serge? His brother?

17) How important are Twelve-Step Programs in the recovery of the main characters in this novel?

18) How has Abel changed by the end of the novel? What choices has he made, and how will those choices affect the lives of those around him?

19) At the end of the novel Abel says, "Sometimes it hurts to think about where I came from. But now I know it's the only way to understand how far I've come." How is this true?

About the Author

HEATHER NEFF is a professor of African-American Literature at Eastern Michigan University and holds a doctorate from the University of Zurich. She is the author of three previous novels, *Blackgammon, Wisdom* (which was named an Honor Book by the Black Caucus of the American Library Association) and the Harlem Moon title *Accident of Birth*. The winner of numerous teaching awards and a popular public speaker, Neff has lived and traveled widely in Europe and the Caribbean.